A King's Wisdom

David S. Longworth

A King's Wisdom is a medieval fantasy novel. All events and characters in this book are fictional. Any historical accuracy is coincidental.

Hardcover ISBN: 978-0-9996809-4-0
Paperback ISBN: 978-0-9996809-2-6
eBook ISBN: 978-0-9996809-3-3

This page is intentionally left blank.

CONTENTS

CONTENTS

For those who choose to live instead of exist

ES SELAMU ALEIKUM

The azure summer sky burned over Starkton, a Lantheon Realm kingdom, quenchable neither by the bodily fluids of her people and livestock nor by the Healing Waters River flowing into Titan Bay. Flowered colognes and perfumes competed with the odors and aromas of Starkton's districts. Enduring the heat and various scents dutifully, Starkton's sentries patrolled the streets and rooftops wearing an ivory surcoat emblazoned with King Gwayne Sterling's silver hare.

Prince Drake, the auburn-haired and amber-eyed son of King Gwayne and Queen Alysse Lilan-Sterling, was the Architecture Master and traversed the city and countryside today in an emerald litter, resting his muscular and bronzed body after paragoning his craftsmen. During his travel, Drake changed into a snow-white shirt and maroon breeches to match Starkton's building colors before the

1

litter stopped on a side road at a white stone manor lined with orange banners bearing a white dragon.

This has to be the correct manor, that's House Wyvern's standard, Drake noted before time froze as a golden-haired woman with purple eyes and square jaw played her lute beside another with a long copper braid and lavender gown, her eyes matching her silver harp. *And right there's Marigold, with famed harpist Sable Wyvern.* He continued watching Sable. *Maybe I can talk Marigold into having a threesome sometime.* As Drake continued watching the ladies play their instruments, Sable entered the manor and returned with a slender man wearing a noble's sapphire and crimson doublet with a short dark beard on his face, thinning umber hair, and silver eyes. As the man approached Prince Drake, the violet spots in his eyes manifested with the stench of cat piss.

"Good afternoon, I am Prince Drake Sterling, Starkton's Architecture Master and son of King Gwayne. Is this residence home to esteemed landlord Richard Wyvern?"

The man sported a crooked yellowing grin and responded, "Yes, milord, I am he. My sister is on the porch playing her harp with lute player Marigold Bilteen."

"I'm *well* acquainted with Marigold, Colette, Rickard, Robert, father General Randall, and worked under mother Jolenta until her death. I've stood upon rooftops near two of your sister's concerts. Do ye have a blacksmith brother named Abelot? Is he inside as well?

"Abelot's either at his smithy or knocking someone around. Has he gotten into trouble again?"

"The Crown has an offer best stated in person, so ride in my litter to the White-Grey Keep although you reek of cat piss."

"Please pardon the stench, milord, my cat isn't housebroken yet. And thank you for the honor; I've never thought myself a lord. My siblings and I grew up as baseborn bastards with my father's surname granted as gestured mercy, but we choose success instead of mediocrity and baseness." He paused. "Say, is this a serious offer, or are ye 'seasonin' the meat before the roast?'"

"There may be roasted venison to devour after ye wash your clothes. Climb in lest I drag you in, ye chamber pot." Richard hesitated before obeying the prince.

During their trip, they passed Alysse's brothel and Abelot's smithy in the dense city limits before transitioning into the forestry and shrubbery of Starkton's countryside leading to the White-Grey Keep. As the prince peeked beyond the curtains, a farmer pushed a wheelbarrow full of manure from a meadow. "That farmer husbands his cattle near the Healing Waters and Cook's Knife rivers flowing near my castle. Look ahead." The men leaned out of the litter. Ahead was the White-Grey Keep's signature granite and marble towers greeting them with admission through the portcullis.

Upon entry to the courtyard, the doughy aroma of the castle's bakery snuffed out all other scents while sparring in the training grounds dampened all other noises. Richard salivated. "I want whatever they're serving today!"

"Later." Drake opened the throne room door. A great hall stabilized by marble pillars patterned with silver diamonds was furnished with aspen-wood furniture, the empty throne at the opposite end bearing silver hares as its head and armrests, silver rabbit feet as the leg ends. "Father?!" Prince Drake's voice echoed through the hallways near the throne. A pale, plump king with a grey beard thicker than the long wisps dangling from his scalp stumbled into the room and spilled burgundy wine from his flagon. Wine stains riddled his argyle turquoise and black silk doublet. "Father, you're drunk during business again?"

King Gwayne could not focus his mismatched amber and green eyes as he responded, "Carpe whatever," raised the flagon to his mouth and drank the nonexistent wine. "You're all wankers, but any lass I see, I spank her! Muahahaha!" The king wet his pants, raised his fists and screamed, "I'M THE KING! MUAAHAHAHAHA!"

Act like it for once. "Yes, you are. Anyhow, I brought Ri-"

"SCRAWNY MAN!" King Gwayne pointed at Richard. "Are you Peter Wyvern's son who built wealth through real estate!?"

"Yes, Your Grace, I am the one you seek."

King Gwayne Sterling smiled with furrowed brows. "Good, my new appointed Treasurer. You now manage the finances of Starkton, the White-Grey Keep, and mine."

"Thank you for this honor, Your Grace. When and where do I start?"

The king leaned forward and retched near the wine puddle.

LAKE

Dawn's peach sunrise unveiled the dust-blanketed furniture and blinded Lord Richard Wyvern awakening hungover from last night's festivities, dizzily rising nude from beneath a wolf and deer pelt blanket to dress himself in his gold paisley-patterned rose doublet, corduroy breeches and black boots. As he pinned his moonstone dragon pin gifted by the Sterlings onto his shirt, he checked the balustrades outside his room. Richard's fetid clothes from yesterday hanged unmolested after two handmaidens washed them late last night.

Richard then searched the desk for all financial records, finding them underneath erotic literature and wax-sealed letters. *This is disgraceful*, he noted as the records stated the castle possessed little-to-no gold and the king had tremendous debts. After notating his suggestions for improvement, Richard relieved himself in the privy, lessening his dizziness, before he returned to grab the records and notes and headed to King Gwayne Sterling.

Ten times larger than the Treasurer's chamber, the king's chamber was walled with animal skulls from Gwayne's hunts, the floor lined with bright rugs from the Elysium provinces, and luxuries filled empty space. King Gwayne lied nude upon his dark wooden bed with two women, one his pale-skinned ginger wife Alysse, the other olive-skinned with black hair.

"Your Grace? Pardon this rude awakening, but this business is urgent. Richard struggled to stare away from the women. All three in the bed stirred.

"Why would you bother me in bed with women?! HAVE YOU NO HONOR?!" the king growled with the ladies glaring in disdain.

I expected the king to get annoyed, but the queen's jade eyes want to tear out my soul. "Forgive me, Your Grace, but I place aside my dignity to fulfill my station."

"If it's worth risking monarchical wrath, I shall honor your business. Leave us, Crystabella." Crystabella obeyed King Gwayne's command by getting dressed and leaving as Richard sat in a nearby oak chair and placed the books in his lap.

Alysse shook her curly auburn hair and scanned Richard Wyvern as he asked "Your Grace, have you neither knowledge nor experience in the art of finance?"

"Money defines who I am," King Gwayne chided.

"Your recklessness is about to bankrupt yourself and the castle, unless a thief has access to the accounts. See for yourself." Richard handed the records to the king and queen.

As Gwayne and Alysse reviewed the records, the queen's face darkened to cabernet wine before she slapped the king. "Are these numbers true, Treasurer?" he cried. "Where can we start turning from bankruptcy to prosperity?"

"We'll begin by saving at least one-fifth, rounded up to the nearest well-rounded hundredth, of all incomes, then split the percentage in half respective to expansion and preservation."

King Gwayne winced. "I thought you were my Treasurer and not my Fool. This foolishness impedes the castle's survival and my lifestyle."

"Saving's not impossible, for even the poor can automate it and never notice their rising treasures."

Alysse smiled and purred, "His words hold merit, Honey." She then leaned over her husband and started shaking Richard's hand. "Thank you for the lecture. Hopefully you will succeed with him where our son and I failed. Inform Starkton's lords as we get dressed."

"You're welcome, and as you wish, Your Grace." Richard left the monarchs and returned the documents before getting a ten year-old steward to bring him Starkton's highest ranked lords. Two and one quarter hours passed before they entered the throne room complaining:

The first was Naval Master Tyrian Sterling, King Gwayne's younger brother whose greying black shags covered an eyepatch over his scarred left eye and brushed his light purple coat; he bore a steel cutlass upon his hip.

Second was the purple-eyed, stout General Randall Bilteen, whose burgundy plated armor bore House Bilteen's topaz fox whereas the silver of his fringed hair and stubble beard on his square jaw matched the sheen of his falchion sword.

Third was the slender, dark-skinned Trade Master Deevon Yor who shaved his head and kept his black beard thick. An immigrant from Pylon on the western coast of the Canteenian Desert across the Elysium Sea, Deevon honored his heritage by wielding a scimitar on his hip and a golden lion pin on his purple coat to honor his distant relatives.

"Thank you all attending this meeting. Even though Prince Drake hasn't arrived yet, we will begin. Due to the shortcomings of the White-Grey Keep, we will start saving one-fifth, rounded up to the nearest well-rounded hundredth, of all incomes and resources on hand. Half of the percentage goes to the castle, the other for your own sector."

Randall Bilteen balled his fist. "Why the taxation? Thinking about following your uncle Cedric?"

Richard remained stoic. "He was a bad fruit on the Wyvern tree. I'm trying to correct the path."

With curtness, Randall answered, "If you betray our trust, you may find yourself as fox meat."

8

A King's Wisdom

As silent tension built between Lord Richard and General Randall, Tyrian left while Deevon stayed and broke it by chiming, "He's right. King Gwayne made him our new Treasurer, and he's giving clear direction a day after appointment. For the soldiers, just give the White-Grey Keep one of every ten recruits and send another to *your* reserves."

Randall growled "Why would I divert ten percent of my army to defend the castle when I can hit our enemies with those same soldiers, and the other ninety percent?" before he darted from the throne room, passing Drake arriving dirty and sweat-drenched.

LEAN

Two blazing summer and windy autumn months passed since Richard Wyvern was named Treasurer of Starkton, and during his second month the White-Grey Keep built a two hundred foot-wide moat funded by his savings strategy. Split by a granite wall into a flowing half beside the castle with waterwheels extending from its mills, and the other half dammed, water flowed into the moat from the Sterling and Drake Channels bent from the Healing Waters and Cook's Knife rivers.

Today he leaned over the balustrade of a new wing's balcony, watching people fish and small ships sail downstream as the clops of racing horse hooves echoed from across the drawbridge into the courtyard. "I'm glad your strategy is working," Tyrian Sterling appreciated from beside him. "Were these new constructs funded with *all* the saved money? This should've cost a lord's treasure."

Bearing a whitened grin, Richard bragged, "I didn't notice how long you've been standing there, but I only used a fourth of the money and resources after reducing expenses. *I focus on the equilibrium between quality and quantity, and reducing expenses without hindering quality of life.* The in-house milling saved an unspeakable amount of gold compared to outsourcing that task, just like when an independent author edits their work instead of hiring an editor."

"What about increasing castle guards?"

"Some of your prince-nephew's construction workers are being trained to become guardsmen."

"How much are you profiting as Treasurer?"

"I agreed to two gold coins annually since I thrive off my real estate investments. Now if you will excuse me, I-" Before Lord Richard could finish his salutation while heading for the nearest door, his sister Sable rushed to them injured with clothes torn and bloodied. "What happened?!"

Sable cried, "Starkton's been attacked, and they tried to rape myself and Marigold!"

Tyrian grabbed his cutlass and snapped, "How many? And where's the prince?"

"Ten-dozen, some in green armor with dragons on surcoats, others in Canteenian clothing. He's severely injured and getting medical attention here at the castle."

"Thank Verítamor you're safe now!" Richard exclaimed.

"Does General Bilteen need reinforcements?" Tyrian asked.

Sable gasped, "No one's seen him, but over sixty of those hellions answered to Abelot's sword."

DEXTERITY

A belot Wyvern edged the rambunctious, stinking crowd. His sapphire eyes, separated by the crooked nose on his shaved face, stared at empty spaces between King Gwayne's guardsmen, the king, and Richard leaning against the back wall. Every time someone bumped into Abelot's long copper hair or House Wyvern orange surcoat with a white dragonhead over his steel armor, he promised death and checked himself. No one dared touch the bastard blade sheathed in the stained leather scabbard on his back, nor his numbing left hand grasping the sheathed rapier pommeled with a moonstone dragonhead mirroring the one on the bastard sword, lest they desired suicide. King Gwayne restored order by gaveling the crowd, silencing everyone before meeting Abelot's gaze. "Renowned blacksmith and warrior Abelot of House Wyvern, state your account of the incident."

Abelot stepped forward. "Y-Y-y-y… Your Grace, I w-w-was working in m-m-m-my shop when p-p-people started screaming. Ten dozen foreigners near th-th… the bay were burning our buildings, attacking, raping, so I grabbed my sword and joined the fight. When I fought to the galley, Tavukish m-m-m-mountain vipers and Pylon sand asps coiled near broken v-vases; th-th-that's what the manifest and captain's log I found claims those snakes were. I c-c-caught one of the scumbags for interrogation. General Bilteen was absent."

King Gwayne responded, "He was here training the latest recruits. Thank you for the information and defending the people, Abelot. Prepare for war."

"Morning Glory will r-r-remain s-s-s-s…surgical, and the forge lit." Abelot held the rapier forward, calling, "Richard, I brought your sword. Do you call it M-Midnight's Arrogance?" A guard retrieved the sword and Richard inspected it. The blade of Midnight's Arrogance was jet-black waved with white notches from shoulder to point.

The king gaveled again and decreed, "Good citizens of Starkton, if you have further business to address, line up where Abelot is standing; otherwise, leave at once. Abelot, you may go." After exiting the throne room with most of the denizens, Abelot sat upon a stone bench near a row of square bushes to ease his mind. A decrepit herbalist crept by carrying fresh rosemary for the castle cooks and doctors, the strong herbal aroma further overloading Abelot's senses. Abelot's peripheral vision blurred, every sound loudened, every smell sharpened, and he started punching the barely-grassed ground while yelling.

Onlookers to Abelot's sensory overload-induced madness gathered, yet none bothered help him until someone struggled to restrain him. "Control yourself, or you'll break your hands again!" a familiar voice cried.

Abelot's knuckles, stinging and dampened, were covered by dented gauntlets. Silence was music, and his meltdown simmered. As Abelot regained his composure he turned to his hero. His brother's silver and violet eyes sparkled in the sunlight. "I'm sorry; it was everything around me again."

Richard hugged his brother. "You did nothing wrong. Wish to get started fulfilling King Gwayne's command?" After Richard escorted Abelot to the training grounds, he armored himself with light leather armor kept on a mannequin and found sparring space. "Ready? Three hits." General Bilteen volunteered to referee their bout before they got the opportunity to unsheathe their swords. Once unsheathed, Morning Glory's bright indigo blade blinded spectators into being unable to see the snow-white fuller and slanted crimson stripes lining the blade. The Wyvern brothers saluted the general, the soldiers, each other, then General Bilteen waved his arm and retreated to begin the bout.

Richard pointed toward Abelot's right shoulder; Abelot swiped away the rapier while wielding his bastard sword one-handed and aimed a punch toward Richard's right cheek, only for Richard to retreat and tap Midnight's Arrogance's point near Abelot's navel.

"One point, Richard."

I'll give him that one, Abelot compromised as he two-handed Morning Glory, closed distance, smacked Richard's rapier away, kicked him to the ground and smirked.

"One-one."

Richard regained battle stance and retreated. As Abelot advanced, Richard aimed at Abelot's right hip and feint the tip around Abelot's parry, but Abelot dodged the attack by lunging left and uppercut Richard with his left hand, bloodying his nose and mouth.

"Two-one, Abelot."

They got back into position, Abelot sweat-free as Richard, sweaty and breathless, advanced and extended Midnight's Arrogance, Abelot answering by binding the rapier with Morning Glory's hilt and jabbing near Richard's navel with a smirk.

"Three-one, Abelot." The brothers shook hands as the spectators, and an impressed General Bilteen, applauded. "Richard, you did better than expected for a number-cruncher."

"My blade work is rusty, General, for I got complacent during peaceful times instead of prepared for war," Richard commented while wiping blood off his face.

Randall nodded. "'tis the downfall of many. *Working on your skills will not only make you better at what you can do, it'll make you more valuable to others who need your abilities.*"

"I've been continuing my education after Abelot and I graduated Zenith Mountain University by reading knowledgeable books intended to enhance one's skills, wellbeing, and income. I like to keep my mind sharper than an executioner's axe."

"Have you gained any new skills since then?"

"Since I moved into the White-Grey Keep, I've been doing carpentry as a productive hobby while fulfilling my duties as a landlord, Starkton's Treasurer, and endeavors I'm not willing to discuss."

Abelot leaned back. *You're repeating the mistake I made when we were teens.* "Brother, a-a-are you sure y-y-you can handle th-th…that workload?"

"Yes, I am determined to succeed wherever I can, and learn from failure."

After Richard re-racked his borrowed armor, Abelot grabbed whetstones and sharpened their blades at a worktable beneath the mango and violet-streaked sunset shadowing Zenith Mountain upstream, unfazed by the time of day and training soldiers.

RIVERS

Y ou're sailing west to the Etauq Empire's capital
Fropilé in Tavuk? To Pylon too?" Richard asked. He
pointed to a white and grey man o'war. "Aboard *Silver
Hare*, the terrorists' galley *The Water Phoenix*, or on one
of the eight frigates?"

Abelot's eye twitched. "Yes, *Silver Hare*, but I d-
d-d...don't know about Pylon," he barked.

"It'll be at least a month or two before you return, and you've
never sailed overseas."

"Th-there's a first f-f-f-f-for everything, brother."

Richard rested his hand upon Abelot's shoulder pauldron,
beseeching, "And a last for everything too. Please, return home
alive." Richard removed his hand and strolled away towards
Starkton's mainland.

A King's Wisdom

As Richard progressed into the city, Abelot remained near Tyrian Sterling's *Silver Hare*, watching stevedores carry large oaken chests to the captain's cabin and supplies down into the hold's storeroom, and then studied *Silver Hare*. Her aspen hull stained by seafoam, faded grey mainsails extending outward, and ram spiked inside its curve alluded a ravenous megalodon ready to hunt.

All banner men of the Green Dragon are our prey, Abelot acknowledged unto himself. *Besides Pylon and Tavuk, could Pañase, Iytal, Mesir, or any other imperial provinces of the Gany continent be involved?* Abelot clasped his gauntleted hands around a crate's edge, leaning upon it as he turned to the recovering city. Construction sounds and the rhythmic ringing of the marbled Verítamor's Blessing chapel carillons created bittersweet music for the priest blessing the chapel's new necropolis. *This could become the biggest war Lantheon has seen since the Elves fought the Goblins before their mutual extinction long ago.*

Goosebumps riddled Abelot's vambraced arms.

Abelot turned around. Captain Tyrian Sterling leaped forward like the hare figurehead at his ship's forepeak as he blurted "BOO! Scare ye?!"

Abelot crossed his arms. "No. Wh-when a paid personal finance publication m-m-m-mistakenly called *you* Davey Sterling years ago, now th-th...that was scary."

Tyrian stepped back. "I beg your pardon?!"

"The s-s-scribe who wr-wrote it f-f-f-found the m-m-m-mistake in its 'Income' s-section *after* the p-p-publication was released."

"Why I oughta..."

Abelot clapped his hands. "He got what he deserved, it didn't sell well…"

Tyrian breathed deep. "Speaking of finances, every ship in this fleet is carrying Starkton goods for trade."

As their conversation continued, Richard arrived with Deevon Yor, the autumn sun luminescing the gilt threading of Deevon's argyle violet and gold doublet. "Good day, Naval Master. Are the ships ready?" Deevon inquired. "The Treasurer and I need to review the manifest before you leave for Fropilé," Deevon remarked before he looked into Abelot's sapphire eyes. "Make sure you bring Starkton Trade Company the best pro-"

"What?! I am also responsible for these goods being shipped!?" Abelot exclaimed.

Deevon stated "indeed Abelot, your brother acquired Starkton Trade Company with me acting as witness for the sale closure. You'll earn commission for supervising the goods and transactions."

Abelot's skin paled. "R-Richard, are you sure you can still juggle your endeavors, this new responsibility too?"

"Yes, and carpentry will be an income-producing hobby. Before I forget, Queen Alysse has an interesting opportunity for us; come with me now." The Wyvern brothers started walking northwest from Titan Bay onto Jester's Fumble until Tyrian began to follow them, Richard shooing him away before they resumed.

During their walk, beggars lined the entertainment district street, receiving handouts and insults; Abelot tossed one a gold coin when no one watched. "What proposition from the q-queen is so important you wanted no company?" he asked as they approached Alysse's Brothel, a large white building, its upper half lined with maroon wall bracings and lower half encased in jagged stone.

"You're not going to believe me if I tell you here and now..." Richard pointed out beneath the entrance's maroon frame stained and engraved with white rabbits. When they entered Alysse's Brothel, the aroma of the stone floor's mint rushes coalesced with coital moans from behind elm-wood doors on each level of the mauve-walled front lobby, its spiraling stairwell in the back left corner. Occupying the lobby's center was a five foot tall marble statue depicting two lovers surrounded by occupied furniture.

While Abelot's eyes followed two women walking past, an olive-skinned in a citrine dress accentuating her cleavage grabbed Abelot's arm. She purred, "Good day, sir knight" as her almond eyes examined Abelot Wyvern head to toe, her beautiful white smile covering her flawless, blushing face. "What would you like today?" she asked without breaking eye contact.

"I'm not-"

Richard interjected "Hello, Crystabella. This is my brother Abelot. We're here to speak with Queen Alysse."

"As you wish," Crystabella saluted before entering a room near the entrance.

Oh, the things I would do to her and those two earlier, Abelot contemplated as he turned back to the statue. "Of all places, why did you bring me to Starkton's grandest brothel?"

"Good afternoon, Lord Treasurer." Abelot turned around. Alysse Sterling greeted them in a magenta gown with her auburn braid leaning over her shoulder.

Richard nodded. "Good day, Your Grace. This is my brother Abelot. We're here to discuss investment in your establishment."

"Oh yes! Come into my office." They walked into her office. Alysse closed the door behind them, everyone sitting in oak chairs matching Alysse's desk.

Richard volunteered, "What would you accept for ten percent of all profits?"

Alysse shifted behind her desk. "Eighty-five thousand gold."

Richard sighed. "Forty-two thousand, five hundred for five percent? Eighty-two thousand for ten percent is our highest offer."

"I'll settle for the eight-two thousand. This transaction is finished."

As Alysse was transcribing the receipt, Abelot reminisced his blacksmithing apprenticeship atop Zenith Mountain and turned to Richard. "How is this fair to her? D-d-d...doesn't she work for her money from here?"

Alysse smiled at Abelot and chimed, "Just like my son, I don't have to... even though I sometimes choose to."

Abelot stared at a letter on Alysse's desk stamped with green wax bearing a dragon. *What's up with that letter?* "Something doesn't fe-feel, um, right. I've always worked f-for my money."

Alysse placed the letter in a desk drawer without breaking eye contact. "Abelot, let not your ego cloud your judgment of this passive income stream which can build unimaginable wealth in due time when combined with other income passive and active incomes." She leaned closer and whispered, "Meditate upon streams feeding rivers, in turn flowing into lakes and oceans. Does their water combined with sunlight not foster the vegetation most life consumes?" She reclined in her chair. "Now you two enjoy the rest of your day."

Richard saluted, "Thank you for this interesting investment opportunity, Your Grace" as the Wyvern brothers stood and nodded to the queen before leaving her office. As they exited the room, Crystabella was standing nearby. Richard grabbed Abelot's shoulder and halted their departure.

"Is something wrong?" Abelot asked.

"Hey Crystabella, Abelot's sailing to the Elysium for a while." Richard then gave her a sack of coins. "What can this get him?"

Smiling, Crystabella led Abelot to a room.

CURVED SHIELD

Storm waves smashed against *Silver Hare* as squalls and gales screamed amidst the thick rainfall south of Pañase's coast. Abelot, pale and sweaty, retched out the captain's cabin window toward a frigate and *The Water Phoenix* concealed by the blanketing rain and nocturnal darkness. "Don't let this experience deter you from sailing open water," the relaxed Naval Master consoled from his cot.

Abelot turned back to the well-lit cabin and almost tripped over his gauntlets and boots before sitting upon his cot. "These waves are t-t-t-t-too harsh for the sh-ships and my stomach-ach. How many will we lose?"

"None if the captains have the smarts to manage the storm tides, and don't you vomit in here or you'll be sleeping somewhere else." Tyrian watched Abelot's failure to sooth his stomach by rubbing his cuirass downward where his digestive tract is located. "I thought you'd bring sleeping clothes."

"This armor has protected and saved me many times."

"There are no threats on this ship, so relax."

"A bed warmer could help me relax."

Tyrian smiled. "That's the spirit!" his applause competed against the loudening squalls. "But if you don't watch out, their feminine daggers can pierce through your cuirass into your heart, and winning a woman's heart is challenging." Tyrian Sterling flipped his hare-engraved silver kukri dagger through his fingers. "Speaking of challenges, I heard your brother challenged you a-."

The squall screams deafened, the lanterns blurred, the cabin's mustiness intensified, and dragon fire scorched Abelot's insides.

Crash!

Abelot fell to the floor flailing his limbs in uncontrollable anxiety and primal rage, growling as the captain leapt off his cot to help him. Tyrian's effort was met with growls and swings. "Abelot?!" he called as the maddening man gazed in viciousness at a lantern. Tyrian extinguished a few, and Abelot's nature eased.

"I'm s-s-sorry, Capt-t-ain. I have brain problem-m-s." Tears rolled from Abelot's stinging eyes. "I don't l-l-l-like crowds, loud noises, strong odors, too much a-t-tention to spr-r-ead."

"I appreciate you letting me know," Tyrian consoled as he hugged Abelot before they returned to their cots.

Gurgle. Gurgle. Abelot rushed to the window and vomited again, forehead fevering as he lied back down and closed his eyes.

Abelot's eyes reopened when a breeze carried a mockingbird's song. He stood behind a sandy castle landscaped with fine fescue darkening with the purpling twilight mottled with narrow magenta clouds. *This is Ashbury Castle in Peasford near Long Harvest*, Abelot noticed. *But why am I here?*

"Bastard," a granite figure called as it approached in silent footsteps and turned into a woman with braided copper hair and silver eyes resembling her hooded tunic and breeches, the dying sunset reflecting off Midnight's Arrogance.

"'Dear' mother Winifred Catrain, what brings you here?" *You hateful, narcissistic cretin whose surname I'm blessed to not have.*

"We must strike your uncle within the shadows. Cedric must pay dearly for his heinous crimes."

Especially for my daily suffering. "Who's paying?"

"It doesn't matter." While the sky darkened, sentries positioned themselves at all entrances while archers took point atop the ramparts and bastions, silhouetted by torches illuminating each sixth crenellation and one in each bastion's corner. "How can we enter?"

"Climb the jutting, uneven bricks."

"But you can't climb in armor."

"Then open a gate for me." Abelot examined the walls. Every brick was plumbed to perfection. "Never mind that idea."

Two guards were stationed outside a portcullis. "I've got one," Winifred responded. "Wait on my lead." One of the guards stepped away to a bush within the dark and pissed. Winifred slipped behind, silenced them, and hid the body while Abelot disguised himself with their armor and assumed their station. Just as the second was beginning to leave, Winifred sliced their throat to the bone, hid the body, and hid in the shadows.

As Abelot peered beyond the gate, a guard captain appeared on the other side and stared him down. "Hey Edric, where's Walder?" they asked. "I thought he went to piss."

Abelot shrugged.

"We need to find him," the captain ordered while opening the portcullis. Just as they stepped outside and noticed the bloodstained earth, Winifred impaled her dagger through the back of their neck. The assassins slipped into the courtyard and reclosed the portcullis. No guards patrolled, but House Wyvern's banners decked the walls.

Winifred rotated her head towards Abelot and whispered, "We should split up. I will check the southwest, you the northeast. That wretch has to be here somewhere."

"I don't like the look of this. Could they be waiting for us?"

"We'll find out soon enough."

After Abelot and Winifred parted ways, Abelot passed a few guards within the interior hallways and gave subtle nods when they acknowledged his presence. Eventually he found an aspen door engraved with wolves. *Is this where Cedric is hiding? Whose sigil is this?* As Abelot contemplated the strange door, his thoughts grew erratic and the door disintegrated into tiny white dragons flying everywhere with silver foxes scurrying the floor. Soft running echoed from the direction opposite his route. Breathless and drenched in blood, Winifred Catrain approached in haste, and thus they entered.

Sitting behind a desk surrounded by treasure was a bald man whose thick dark mutton chops contrasted his brass armor. *No caged, perfumed children?* Abelot noted. "Uncle Cedric, it's 'good' to see you again." Abelot unsheathed Morning Glory and pointed its tip at Cedric. "It'll be even better to see your death end you dragging the Wyvern name through pig dung."

Cedric taunted, "Behold, a knuckleheaded bastard hiding behind his whore mother's skirt! How did my guards fail their duty?"

Blood dripped off Midnight's Arrogance as Winifred purred "I killed your men when I found them drunk in the mess hall passing around the kitchen wench. No one is left to save you." A toothy smile blossomed within her small pink lips.

Cedric revealed the longsword hidden on his lap when he stood. "I should have strangled Abelot after I-."

"There is no honor in betrayal for selfish short-term gain," Abelot growled. The candlelight reflecting off Morning Glory brightened. "I am a white dragon in this world of darkness, protector of the defenseless, banisher of evil. Prepare to die, wretch!" Abelot directed while starting his advance.

"I owe you a warrior's death, but Winifred will be my soldiers' broodmare!" Cedric promised as he swung his longsword and missed Abelot when he ducked. Before Abelot could arise, Winifred rushed Cedric and stabbed him in the opening under his right arm, forcing Cedric to swing at her. Abelot rammed Morning Glory through Cedric's skull as he rose, only for Cedric to scream in repetition "Wake up, Abelot! Wake up!"

Abelot's eyes opened again. Tyrian Sterling was yelling in his face before sprinting sword in hand into the white fog beyond the cabin door. Abelot scurried to finish getting armored and armed preceding meeting Tyrian on deck. Every ship surrounded smoking wreckage as shipmates crowded and studied the fog. "What's g-g-g…going on, Captain?!" Abelot asked.

"Pirates attacked last night. So far it seems they sank one frigate and most likely hauled off her cargo on a schooner flying the Pañase standard sailing west towards Pylon. It's too fast for any of our ships, so those goods are as good as gone. We were able to surround their brigantine and toss flaming pitch onto her hull, killing most except the suicidal fools who boarded *Silver Hare* for us to slaughter except the one we caught. You and I slept so hard we missed the battle."

I had a battle of my own last night, my umpteenth nightmare. "How bad of a c-c-c-c-commercial loss d-d-d-d…did their raid cause?"

"We split each merchant's cargo across each ship in case something like this was to happen, so ten percent per merchant. We can increase pricing to try to recuperate the loss."

Abelot yawned. "And where's th-the pirate you m-m-m-mentioned?"

Tyrian pointed to the foremast. "Let him wake you up."

Abelot nodded to the captain, rushed to the brown-bearded pirate and cracked his ribs. The pirate howled with blooded spittle. "Who sent you?"

"Bugger off!" The pirate yelled.

Not removing his gauntlet beforehand, Abelot decorated the deck with the pirate's teeth and held his head to stare into his hazel eyes. "Who ordered this attack?"

"Bugger off, sword-swallower!" The pirate spat blood onto Abelot's armor and surcoat.

Abelot looked to the others and uttered "I need a dagger to teach this punk about life without *his* sword." Tyrian handed Abelot his dagger while the crewmembers pulled down the pirate's pants and exposed his manhood.

"WAIT! It was a small, scrawny woman in Fropilé! She wore a green and gold hooded cloak, gemstones in her dagger and bow!" Tears filled the pirate's eyes. "Geld me not!"

"Thank you, but your presence is too risky, so I'll let Verítamor decide your fate." Abelot then grabbed the pirate by his shoulder and carved deep incisions along his torso, blood gushing all over Abelot's armor before the sailors painted *Silver Hare*'s deck sanguine as they dragged and tossed the pirate overboard.

THE COIN

Smoke and mist blanketed the murky grey sky over the Elysium Sea as ashes and embers emulated peaceful snowfall and naval warfare debris littered the water. However, among the ruins was a paling sailor staring into the heavens, weeping "Verítamor?! Dubuver?! Xyn?! Leggelius?! Why did you let demons torment meh? ANSWER ME!" through his injured mouth as his gashed chest bled. "A beast left me to feed sharks. If a higher power exists and is listening, is this truly my end? Have midays been spent in vain? I only wanted riches and wine in this life."

The brigantine *Riches and Wine*, accompanied by an aged schooner, hid like a bedbug within the violent storm of the pitch black night before. Within *Riches and Wine*'s hull, merry fellows drank exquisite spirits and sang while cleaning their battle worn weapons, counted gold, and bragged about bedding the schooner's women. A couple seadogs retched into buckets, prompting the inebriated sailor atop deck volunteering to man the sails. As the drunkard toiled, the tattoo-headed, leather-skinned ship captain accosted him, wearing about his neck a golden chain adorned with dragon-shaped emeralds and an eye patch covering his left eye.

"Ahoy, Captain Nolryk Doran, what brings ye 'ere this hour? I'da thought ye'd be downstairs or beddin' your wench." *That's what I'd rather be doing, oh riches and wine.* He stared at Captain Nolryk's magnificent jewelry and covered his nauseous stomach.

Nolryk adjusted the chain. "I'm pleased you're not neglecting humble duties with the layabouts, Múto, yet I smell moonshine on you. Spotted any ships?"

"Nothing yet, but me vision's a little hazed from the cups. Again, what's the green woman with the bow and dagger payin' for Lantheon?" Múto staggered to the railing, vomited into the ocean and pissed through the railing.

"Thirty gold per person, but I got my new medallion."

Múto stashed his manhood and wiped vomit from his beard. "I'd rather bed her and pluck the gemstones from her weapons."

Nolryk drew a dagger and promised "Careful, lest I *silence-*"

A ragged man rushed to the captain, pointing towards the foremast. "Ships ahead, Captain." he claimed.

Nolryk stowed his dagger and studied the distance through his looking glass. "Well I'll be damned! That's the legendary Tyrian Sterling's *Silver Hare* leading a fleet."

"Ye sure?" the ragged sailor inquired. "I can't read squiggles, lines, and dots."

"Before becoming Starkton's Naval Master, Tyrian was Starkton's emissary to Etauq Emperor Augulan Ventneir, the father of Joaquin and grandfather of our current emperor Septimius. For three decades Tyrian sacked and pillaged open waters, bribing his leftovers to Lantheon and Etauq before his brother Gwayne named him Starkton's Naval Master to prevent him turning against Starkton; but I believe Gwayne was jealous Tyrian could've conquered many islands and crowned himself king." Captain Nolryk pointed to the fleet. "Ye see the flag and fierceness of his man o' war?" he asked when handing Múto his looking glass.

It makes barely any good when my vision's blurred, oh riches and wine. "Captain, you think we could get a good bounty of riches and wine from Tyrian's fleet?"

"One frigate's worth, then flee before they catch us."

Using the pirate's ideal veil, Captain Nolryk's brigantine and schooner sailed into the fleet undetected. Once a frigate was chosen, Múto and twelve other pirates maintained stealth and plundered it as the skyline started sheening with the dissipating rain and a white, misty fog formed. Múto pissed into the sea again and returned to *Riches and Wine* sober. "This wooden fish was a good catch," Múto reported to Nolryk. They gazed upon *Silver Hare* dwarfing *Riches and Wine*. "Feel like catching a legend?"

Captain Nolryk's visible black eye sparkled as he hissed "Why not? If we die today, then it's as legends. ALRIGHT MEN, RAISE

THE FLAG, SINK THIS FRIGATE, AND ONTO THE MAN O' WAR!"

"Captain, we could add any number of these ships to your fleet and-."

"I don't care!" Nolryk blurted as *Riches and Wine*'s trebuchets flung flaming tar-covered bearings at the frigate, boarded the schooner and raised Pañase's magenta water lily on green and yellow stripes, and the ruffians boarding *Silver Hare* were greeted with alarms and being outnumbered seven-to-one.

Is this where my story ends? Múto wondered as he battled countless enemies before reaching the captain's cabin. Once inside the cabin, a shaggy black-headed man slept in one cot whilst in another cot tossed and turned, as if enduring a nightmare, an armored second man bearing long wavy copper hair and a crooked nose. *Should I kill them before they draw swords?*, Múto wondered amidst the chaos of naval warfare. Euphoria spread head to toe as Múto was compelled to whisper "No" and turned back to the deck and rushed to feminine screams across the railing. While *Riches and Wine* was sinking with Captain Nolryk's schooner gone, some female prisoners drowned while others clung to burning wreckage and singed alive. *No one is saving them*, Múto acknowledged before turning back to the massacre of his fellow stragglers. Euphoria overtook him again as his enemies turned their blades to him, he tossed down his cutlass, and was tied to the foremast. *Is someone going to save me?*

The black-headed man in the cabin stepped out and communed with a sailor. *What's my fate, and is he the legendary Tyrian Sterling?* Múto wondered once the man stepped back into the cabin. After "Wake up, Abelot! Wake up!" was audible from within the cabin, the armored man appeared soon after and communed with Tyrian. *It must be, and his name must be Abelot*, Múto acknowledged as Abelot approached and cracked his ribs.

"Who sent you?" Abelot inquired.

"Bugger off!" Múto yelled.

Not removing his gauntlet beforehand, Abelot decorated the deck with Múto's teeth and held his head. Golden ethereal wings reflected behind Abelot as sunlight pierced the fog and gilt his steel armor. "Who ordered this attack?"

This proud prick must think he's some sort of savior. Does a savior return mercy with brutality? "Bugger off, sword-swallower!" Múto spat blood onto Abelot's armor and insulting surcoat.

Abelot looked to the others and *taunted* "I need a dagger to teach this punk about life without *his* sword." Tyrian handed Abelot his dagger while the crewmembers pulled down Múto's pants and exposed his manhood.

Monsters, the lot of them. "WAIT! It was a small, scrawny woman in Fropilé! She wore a green and gold hooded cloak, gemstones in her dagger and bow!" Tears filled the pirate's eyes. "Geld me not!"

"Thank you, but your presence is too risky, so I'll let Verítamor decide your fate," Abelot *purred* as he grabbed Múto by the shoulder and carved deep incisions along his torso, blood gushing all over Abelot's armor before the sailors painted *Silver Hare*'s deck sanguine when dragging and tossing Múto overboard.

Verítamor, if you exist and are listening, save me or let me die in peace.

"ABELOT! TYRIAN! LET MY PERSISTENCE BE THE ANSWER TO YOUR VICIOUS SENSE OF HONOR!" Múto exclaimed as he reopened his eyes to a full moon lighting the starless night.

Verítamor blessed me with peace.

Yet the moment of peace passed when rough waves washed Múto underwater. As he swam to the surface, the moon was eclipsed by charred wood… and fishtailing fins.

THE CONDUCTOR

Seagull squawks and harmonious voices created a chorus invigorating the tepid autumnal air of Fropilé's docks as Abelot and Tyrian supervised Fropilé's stevedores unloading the trade goods and transporting north through the red and yellow clay city six caged wagons, concealing behind banners showing a green dragon on a golden field, green-armored gorillas. "Abelot," Tyrian uttered as he pointed with a drooping black sleeve to a two-wing, hundred-pillared structure balustrading the city and northeastern Verítamor's Vow plains, a tholos atop both towers. "The Regemarce is where we seek audience with Emperor Septimius, but we need an official to give proper introduction lest he think to send *our* heads back to Starkton instead of those we seek."

"A-a-are you sure th-th-th-that's the correct b-b-b-building, milord?" Abelot pointed to a twenty-towered building a mile south of the Regemarce. "That looks more significant."

"Yes, I've sailed here plenty before. The Regemarce is the political center, and that basilica's called Verídom. And before you ask, the Regemarce's secondary wing is the Royal Library. Now find someone in the Ruby and Emerald Bazaar while I finish supervising before you annoy me."

"Thank you for the information."

Abelot ventured into the city on russet stone pathways, aiding along the way an elderly bronzed woman in a full-body mantle with a pointed right shoulder by loading her groceries onto a small cart in exchange for directions, following the congestion of finer dressed citizenry. When he reached the Ruby and Emerald Bazaar, it covered over one hundred thousand square feet, had large ruby and emerald chunks embedded in saffron stucco, and hundreds of shops. But along the exterior was an innovative smithy peddling armory engraved with patterns on some, animalistic appearances on others, crossbows, and weaponry designed to launch metal rounds.

A plump bronzed man wearing a sleeveless and hooded leather tunic toiled with a marigold battle axe engraved with ivory gorillas growling holstered on his back. "Greetings, fellow blacksmith" Abelot hailed. The man paused working and turned his russet eyes towards Abelot, sweat dampening his thick, frosted black beard and short hair. "Y-y-your w-work is impressive, but m-m-m-m-my sh-ship captain and I are h-h-here on d-d-d-d-d-…diplomatic matters and request an off-f-f-ficial escort to the-to the Regemarce. Who can help us?"

In a profound husky accent, the blacksmith stated, "I, Cahít Andíno, supply the emperor's Sanguine Guard with quality steel. You look like someone I met long ago. Have you shopped here before?"

"No,"Abelot responded as he unsheathed Morning Glory, continuing "but here's my sword" as he handed it shining with magnificence to Cahít. "I did not forge th-th-th…this, but maintain it."

"I never expected to see Morning Glory again, nevertheless in excellent condition. I sold this sword and a rapier I named Midnight's Arrogance many moons ago to a foreigner from Starkton or something like that if I'm recalling correctly."

"I'm h-h-h-his son Abelot. M-m-my br-br-brother R-Richard holds Midnight's Arrogance."

"It's a small world!" Cahít pointed behind him and asked "See that sword over there?" Mounted on the back wall was a dark crimson bastard sword with a deep cobalt fuller, ultramarine V-shaped stripes, and golden quillons curved towards the onyx grip. "That is Hadlia, the kindred spirit to Morning Glory. I named our swords after local flowers." He then returned Morning Glory to Abelot.

"Are you going to help me?" Abelot asked.

"Yes, but it will be a while since I have many projects needing fulfillment."

"I can forge tough steel."

Cahít studied Abelot's armor. "Your armor pales to my wares. Do you know how to damascene metal?"

"I'm willing to learn."

"Enter."

Abelot entered Cahít Andíno's workstation and apprenticed for three hours before Tyrian Sterling approached the counter with Starkon's evidence. "What do you think you're doing, Abelot?!" Tyrian asked. "We don't have the time for this."

As Cahít was turning to Tyrian, he growled "Paying the price for audience with Emperor Septimius, and excelling under my tutelage. You must be the captain he mentioned earlier. My name is Cahí-"

"Moving on up in the world, eh, Cahít? Long time no see." Tyrian responded before leaning forward and continuing their conversation in whispers. Once they finished whispering, Tyrian saluted, "Thank you, Cahít. Find me at the docks, in the bazaar, or at a nearby brothel" before parting.

Another hour passed, and the blacksmiths' workload finished after the whitened morning sunshine yellowed for the afternoon. As they were tidying the workstation, Abelot pointed his right hand towards a silver-swirled topaz kukri dagger with a magenta grip, inquiring, "Cahít, b-b-b-b-before we leave, I'd like to buy th-that d-d-d-d-dagger f-f-f-f-for my sister; how much is it?"

"Betrothal to her."

"Then I'll pass."

"Relax, and learn how to take a joke. Four-hundred gold, and her name is Eloquence. For an extra hundred, I'll also sell you a blacksmithing book containing my techniques."

"Done." Abelot exchanged five-hundred gold coins for Eloquence and the book before Cahít locked the smithy, Abelot holstered the dagger on his right hip, and they got lunch from a bakery and winery before finding Tyrian shopping fine garments.

"S-s-s-s-s-seems like my brother needs t-t-t-to mentor you too," Abelot chimed at the waffling captain.

"And you need speech therapy. Let's get to the Regemarce before Septimius is done 'emperor-ing' for the day." The men trekked to the capitol and entered the emperor's palace through the palace yard rampart's sheltered walkway skirting a ponded garden.

Although the palace exterior was vibrant, the only colors present in the white marbled throne room were on the sanguine and green guards facing each other across the throne room and the meek servant standing near the stairway behind the throne, who then approached the visitors.

"Greetings, Cahít," they announced before turning to Tyrian and greeting him too. "How may I assist you today? Another delivery?"

"These Starktonians are here on diplomatic business."

The servant ascended the stairs and returned, marshalling into the throne room an olive-skin man in burgundy and gold checkered armor whose lustrous black mane was crowned with an olive-branch, and a hazel-eyed bronze woman with sun-gilt copper curls wearing an ivory dress beneath her gilt emerald cloak pinned with a moonstone dragonhead brooch. The servant announced, "Behold, Septimius Ventneir, Emperor of the Etauq Empire, and Carillon Doran, Queen of Pylon and daughter of Queen Mother Agnes."

Everyone bowed before the emperor and rose at his command. "State your business, visitors from Starkton" Septimius commanded. As Tyrian was recapitulating the attack in Starkton and the piracy, he presented the evidence, darkening Septimius' complexion. "I have no choice but to respond to these acts of war, My Grandfather's Emissary. Guards, arrest her!"

Septimius' Sanguine Guard surrounded Carillon while her guards drew their weapons as she answered "Dubuver forewarned me of this wrongdoing you will answer for. Guards, defend your queen."

Two Sanguine Guards shielded Emperor Septimius while everyone else fought. Cahít severed a Queen's Guard's arm, knocked away another one's spear then broke their nose with a head-butt. *He can handle himself*, Abelot decided while fighting a scimitar-wielder and one with a halberd. *But what about Tyrian?* A white and green flash ducked and darted beyond Abelot's opposition as Tyrian joined Abelot's duel and called out "Get her, or our tribulations up to now will be for nothing!"

Abelot pursued Carillon, but his encumbrance increased halfway into his sprint, every step he and Carillon took imitating hammers pounding on metal, copper flavoring filling his mouth. His sprint slowed to a jog with visions of hammering luminescent red metal and dipping it into water filling his mind. *I overworked myself*, Abelot acknowledged as the distance between them grew. *I cannot catch her. The people of Starkton will never forgive me, not even my sis…*

That's it!

Abelot reached to his right hip and unsheathed his sister's dagger, peripheral vision blurring as he aimed Eloquence and slung it when Carillon slowed near the garden door.

"Mace!" Carillon cried before blood spewed from Eloquence's impalement in her cervical spine. As Carillon drowned in her own blood, many guardsmen lied dead as Septimius' surviving Sanguine Guards and reinforcements took the remaining Queen's Guards into custody.

Emperor Septimius Ventneir held up a hand and decreed, "Although you Starktonians came to me as strangers, you leave today as allies who unveiled my subordinate's treachery. Thank you, and I assure Starkton shall get retribution, and I especially thank you for serving the Etauq Empire once again, My Grandfather's Emissary."

"You're welcome, Your Majesty" Tyrian responded with a bow.

Abelot looked into Septimius' eyes. "Ex-x-cuse me, Your Majesty, b-b-b-but we an-n-n-n-n-n-n…anticipated returning home with at-t-t-t least one facilitator's head." He looked at Carillon's body. "May Starkton have her head, Your Majesty?"

"Yes. Also, I do need to confiscate *The Water Phoenix* since it is further evidence of Pylon's war crimes." Tyrian agreed while Abelot decapitated the deposed queen's carcass and wrapped the head with her cloak. "Cahít, you have helped me many times in many ways, friend. Thank you."

"You're welcome, Your Majesty. I knew the dragon-god Dulcimort deceived Carillon the moment she referred to it as Dubuver." Cahít nodded, and then left the throne room with the travelers.

"But wh-wh-why was her last w-word 'mace?'" Abelot asked when they stepped into the garden and a dragonfly flew at him. Abelot swung at it, missed, turned to hit it…

And paused with goosebumps riddling him as the older bronze woman he passed that morning reappeared, wearing a gilt green hooded cloak fastened by an ornamental dagger, bearing a matching bow upon her back instead of a deformed right shoulder.

TRACELESS

"Y ou requested my presence, Your Graciousness?" *Is this about yesterday, or just an ordinary order?* Cahít's voice echoed throughout the empty throne room lined with the black and red banners of the Etauq Empire illuminated by a burgundy sunset, a toothy grin filling his frosted black beard. *Even Verítamor recognizes our triumphs in these harsh times.* "Whoever cleaned the answer to Queen Carillon's treason yesterday did an excellent job." He pointed to the banners. "And I like your new decorations. I hope you paid the housekeepers well." *Where are your guards in a time like this?* "Your Majesty, is the rolled parchment in your hand the guards' measurements? New armor for yourself?"

Emperor Septimius remained stoic while pronouncing "My dear friend, I cannot be grateful enough for the blessings granted through your work" and glanced to the sunset as he descended the dais. "But today, I shine light upon darkness. Based upon the evidence against House Doran, I fret they are conspiring secession or conquest, and yesterday's conclusion only decapitated one head of their hydra; Prince Davirius is next in succession to Pylon's throne, Nolryk still plagues the Elysium Sea, Agnes is slithering within the dark, and Mace is lurking somewhere in Lantheon." Septimius planted his hand upon Cahít's shoulder. "Today, I request not just any weapon or armor, Cahít Andíno, but for the blade of your unwavering loyalty to excise the aberrant within Pylon. Can you fulfill this order?"

"My axe is yours, Your Gloriousness."

"Excellent. Begin with Davirius, the most strategic target." Emperor Septimius gave Cahít the sealed scroll. "This is for the court of Pylon, preferably my emissary Eli Praes. Make haste before Davirius can counterattack" the emperor commanded before sending him away.

Darkness fell upon Fropilé's russet stone streets and grassed sand, furnace embers still lighting the smithy walls and intricate metalwork as Cahít concealed his wares. "How am I going to sneak into Pylon?" Cahít asked himself as he locked the smithy to begin his mission… until his axe holster lightened.

Cahít turned around to an old woman in a gilt green hooded cloak fastened by an ornamental dagger with a matching bow upon her back sprinting as his heavy axe hit the ground. "Why you…!" he yelled while grabbing the axe, chasing her until she disappeared near the harbor. "Where in the Battlemage's name did she go?!" he gasped while scanning the area.

As Cahít caught his breath, green-armored soldiers played dice with wagered gold near a ship bearing House Doran's flag. *There's no way Doran soldiers are here in the city, unless that's how their queen got here,* Cahít thought while creeping closer. The scents of beer and mead emanated from them and flagons as barrels lined the dock.

Should I tell the emperor, or see what I can do?

A stout soldier pissed over the harbor's edge before refilling his flagon, losing all his money at the dice game, and staggering up the ramp to the deck. Cahít followed him into the hold, watched from the shadows as the man undressed and retired amidst others slumbering, snatched his armor and snuck off the ship undetected.

COMMITMENT

*D*id two months actually pass since Abelot left? Richard Wyvern contemplated as snowflakes descended from the ivory heavens, admiring their geometry as he twiddled the rolled letter in his hand, unsealed its orange seal and read it:

Dear Richard,

As you requested, I have been managing Starkton Trade Company and your rental properties. Although they are earning money, there are tremendous debts hindering their potential. When could we amortize those debts so those incomes can become more profitable, Treasurer of Starkton?

Love, Sable.

Richard looked to the clutter on his oak desk, the dusty rapier beside it, and wept. *I made this problem*, he thought to himself before studying his woodwork of the desk and matching bedframe. *And I can*

make the solution. Maybe the completion of my business today will ease my mind.
Richard set two sealed documents aside, pinned his white dragon
brooch onto his orange fur cloak with puffed sleeves, holstered the
rapier to his left hip, grabbed the documents and exited the room.

As Richard strode towards the master quarters, Gwayne's voice
reverberated from the throne room, where he found him bundled in
his vanilla fur coat meeting with nobility smelling of mint. "Your
Grace..." Lord Richard started. The sundry sneered in silence when
he continued, "I have been seeking you. Who are these men?"

A slender, bald-headed man in a claret doublet and gilt emerald
cloak fastened with a topaz dragon brooch chimed "We are here in
exigence to speak with King Sterling on private matters," while
chewing mint and stroking the pointed, frosted gold beard beneath
his hazel eyes. "Now, if you don't mind..."

"I'm Starkton's Treasurer here to discuss official business,
Stranger."

"You're the perfect official for our discussion then. My name is
Mace Doran, hailing from Honet's capital bank." The hilt of his
sheathed dagger and longsword shone. "We're here to discuss the
king's debts."

"What a coincidence, I'm here for the same reason."

"King Gwayne has been repaying his arrears with loans from
various banks, foregoing some payments, and debts he cosigned are
defaulting."

"I am aware and assure you great improvements will be made towards strengthening the king's relationship with you all. Certainly we can come to some arrangements."

Mace Doran's face displayed content, but his eyes did not. "Splendid. Our client needs to avoid catastrophic financial failure if the wellbeing of he and his son is to continue."

Why did he exclude Queen Alysse? "Be glad I understand your statement just now wasn't a threat our king and prince, lest you be cut down" Richard barked while tapping the hilt of Midnight's Arrogance.

"It is a simple unavoidable truth… and nothing more."

Everyone turned towards King Gwayne spilling and drinking wine from the golden, emerald-encrusted chalice in his left hand as Richard cleared his throat and addressed, "Your Grace, you entrusted me with fixing you and the castle's finances, and I am doing my best to meet expectations; however, you still engage in habits needing an immediate end, and *the only person who can make the choice is you.* Your debts mostly originate from your extravagant lifestyle pampering your ego."

Gwayne sipped, rebutted "You have debts too, Treasurer" and sipped some more.

"Yes, I admit I too have debts to pay, my student loans and business debt granted me the financial leverage to obtain valuable knowledge and wisdom applicable for gainful employment and the exponential amplification of my businesses' income. *The only three debts anyone could ever need as leverage for success are student loans, business debt, and mortgages. Accumulating debt to fund a lifestyle and cosigning for loans is foolishness only favoring money lenders.*" When Gwayne turned away in shame, Mace glared in silence. "You need to balance living in the future and the present when building wealth and with life in general. Does my counsel make sense, Your Grace?"

King Gwayne wept, "My ignorance was limiting my potential and overcommitting me. I swear upon Drake's life to correct my behavior today."

Mace and the other financiers watched Gwayne finish his wine and whine. "Thank you for your cooperation, Treasurer. If he keeps his word then Starkton will be in good standing with us."

"You're welcome, Mister Doran."

As the bankers left the throne room, Richard gave his documents to Gwayne before embracing winter's chill and the innumerable tumbling snowflakes in the snow-covered courtyard. Under the bakery's eave sat Mace on a dry bench recording notes, chewing mint leaves, and basking in the scents of the wood smoke billowing from the bakery's chimney and the bakery's bread and pies. Richard trudged through the snow to him.

"Mister Doran, do you need to discuss in depth Starkton and King Gwayne's accounts with you?"

Mace's hazel eyes sparkled as he changed focus to Richard. "We can, but in warmth and with food in our bellies."

"Good idea." They entered the White-Grey Keep's balmy, aromatic bakery and watched the bakers work before Richard ordered an iron skillet-fried apple pie with a Starkton sweet red whereas Mace ordered a blueberry pie and mint cookies with white zinfandel. Once their meals were ready, the men went to a table and began their feast.

Mace ate a slice of his blueberry pie and washed it down. "I never heard you mention your name."

"Richard of House Wyvern." He broke the crisp, golden-edged crust of his apple pie as part of a slice and embraced the seasoning of the skillet mixing with the sweetness of the apples as he ate.

"A Wyvern, huh?" Mace ate a cookie. "By any chance are you kin to Leggeron?"

"Indeed the legendary Leggeron the Stern was my grandfather. He was named after some god the Grecans or Namorians worship in their polytheistic religion, and I'm sure if that god exists then it's proud of Leggeron's goblin extinction."

"I'm surprised you've forgotten Namor is Greca's capital since Greca technically borders the Starkton province within the Three Seasons Forest, unless you're amongst those who believe Grecan territory begins beyond the forest's northwest perimeter." Mace sipped his wine. "Anyway, I met that vagrant when he stormed into my bank accusing me of cheating Peter and Cedric and disemboweled three guards as he escaped his arrest."

"This is the first I'm hearing of this."

"Do you deny him choosing the Latran Wolves over his family?" Richard remained silent.

"Whoever withheld it wished you not follow Leggeron's example."

Tell that to Abelot. Richard finished his pie before Mace ate seven-tenths of his. "Let's get to business." He sipped his sweet red. "Show me the accounts."

Mace handed him the account book and ate another mint cookie. "How do you propose the debts should be handled?"

"When I accrued educational debt in multiple loans, I promptly eliminated the smallest loan while paying minimal payments on the larger ones, and when it was amortized, I did the same thing with the next smallest but saved the money that would have gone towards the previous. Some people stack the payments after a debt is paid, but that eliminates the ability to increase one's money on hand."

"Brilliant." Mace's eyes sparkled. "Care to finish the rest of my wine?"

"What the drunk don't know won't hurt him," Richard commented before finishing Mace's white zinfandel.

Mace smiled. "Since our business today has concluded, we best be on our way."

"Safe twavvel" Lord Richard slurred.

Mace nodded in return.

As they were exiting the bakery, ten masked assailants fought the throne room's courtyard entrance guards around five tipped wagons.

Richard staggered behind one assailant and impaled their heart, yet another stabbed Richard between his right ribs. He then challenged his stabber, failed his parry and was stabbed again while closing distance to crush their windpipe. Mace Doran and the guards killed all but two. As the guards surrounded one after they slit a guard's throat, Richard and Mace challenged the other, only for Richard to get impaled through his navel while Mace slew them.

Richard fell into the ivory slush, feeling it and his wounds heat up while the rest of his body cooled. He examined the temperature change. His blood darkened and melted the snow as his skin color disappeared. "Guards, find a doctor and King Gwayne!" Mace cried over Richard yet applied no pressure upon any wound. Snowflakes fell into Richard's eyes, their geometry blinding and stinging.

Richard blinked and found himself strolling in a light snowfall amidst the edifices of Zenith Mountain University with a bag full of books shielding his back, a fat sack of gold on his waist, and beautiful female students glancing.

"Richard! Pl-Please…" a voice called from the direction of the library. He followed the voice, found the library and entered.

The library was dim, but Richard located a seat on the quietest floor, lit a candle, and began studying *The Prosperous Lord*. As he studied, an older man identical to Richard but with grey hair and sapphire eyes sat nearby.

"Father? Or do you prefer Peter?"

He whispered "I'd prefer you live well and continue studying."

"I intend to live well by ignoring the advice and demands of miserable, unambitious fools. I hope you're proud."

...FOR ALL

Pandemonium bellowed from the thousands-congested Lion's Den as fourteen armed combatants and seven hungry lions battled in the sandstone arena. Despite the shaded comfort of the podium, the sweat in Davirius Doran's sun-dyed copper curls dampened the celadon doublet under his golden cuirass. "You want to bet who gets to live?" Davirius wheezed while twisting the tip of his soul patch into a point. "Thirty on the trash," he declared while depositing coins into an elaborate vase beneath the long table.

Salted russet dust swept into the podium and spoiled Eli Praes' grapes and bleu cheese. "Thirty on the slaves and gladiators," Eli purred before tossing in his bet and calling a passing servant to bring more sustenance and braid his straight black hair. "Anything for you, Duchess?"

Although Marilyn Yor's almond eyes studied Eli's smooth gold face and imperial mantle; her mind's eye studied Pylon's reddened marble pyramids, sandstone Dragon's Roost palace and Lion's den, mudstone buildings and the Elysium Sea's tide ebb the Canteenian Desert. She rasped "lions," her wrinkled almond skin tingling in ecstasy, when a disemboweled criminal screamed as a lion started eating him and one of Eli's fallen. Marilyn swung her silvering dreadlocks behind her blue-violet dress, slipped her gold into the vase and sipped her dark wine as she stared into Davirius' piercing hazel eyes.

"Your ancestors were geniuses to carve the Lion's Den!" Eli exclaimed. "Tell me, why do the people choose to pay your high pricing over street shows and brawls?"

Marilyn sipped more wine. *Justice, mindless entertainment, and love for my family.*

But before the duchess could respond, Davirius volunteered "Distraction from the imperial blemish on Pylon's thousand-year political system, and repaying our debt to Mace."

Marilyn placed her wine on the table. *Foolish boy, you're nowhere nearly as cunning as your brother.* "Please speak no treason, my young prince; the Etauq Empire supports your sister just like the other subordinate monarchs. Indeed our citizens have endured hardships these past couple years, but we're recovering and bettering."

"My cousin and queen mother seek aid for our recovery."

"By that, you mean pillaging other territories and raping their women? I've spoken with wayfarers."

Davirius' face blackened, and he jumped from his seat. "You dare slander House Doran?! Remember your place before you're thrown into your own death pit, hag."

Eli watched three felons get mauled and one cut a lion's throat. "Oh please shut up lest I pay these guards to toss you both in." A gladiator impaled a criminal. "The criminal body count is five. Looks like your coin's becoming ours."

Before Davirius could leave when the final two criminals were eaten by lions, a large bronzed guard with a frosted black beard carrying a letter approached alongside a skittish boy. "Your Grace," he announced in a profound husky accent. "I have a letter from Emperor Septimius, and this messenger is also here for you."

Davirius scowled. "Then let him speak first, and you should have said 'm'lord' instead of 'your grace.' Begin, child."

"A captain named Nolryk s-says he has returned with g-g..goods, but fell short of better haul. He wants forgiveness."

"So the soured dolphin sends a boy instead of seeking forgiveness in person?" Davirius palmed his face and shook his head. "I'll grant it, and tell him his pay will be a new ship and two camels."

"Yes, Mister Grace."

Davirius leaned to the boy's eyelevel. "I'm not a king. The correct salutation when addressing kings and queens is 'your grace.'"

"Forgive me, milord." The child left just before the guard handed the letter, turned away, unsheathed the battle axe and rested its top points on the ground. Davirius read the letter.

"Our 'beloved' emperor and Starkton's Naval Master had my sister and her guards murdered when she was wrongly accused of treason over an attack on Starkton and tried to escape." Davirius wept.

Eli blurted "I am sorry for your loss, Your Grace, but Carillon implied guilt when she chose fleeing over a trial, and if your mother sent those troops…"

"Unbelievable. Pylon shall secede and collect the liar's head."

Marilyn finished her wine and cried, "You have my condolences, King Davirius, but please accept their fate before you bring Pylon's destruction."

The guard turned to the king and intervened, "She's right. You will die against the empire."

Davirius' face further darkened as he screamed "HOLD YOUR TONGUE!"

"Will do." He amputated Davirius' arm at the shoulder.

STRINGS & BARS

How much gross profit is Abelot's expedition going to bring?" *How much am I getting?* Sable asked Marigold Bilteen while strumming her silver harp beside the fireplace in Starkton Trade Company's snow-covered shack near the docks. Sable's cleavage emphasized by the ermine collar of her fuchsia dress remained chill, yet Marigold was unfazed within the fox-pelt cloak covering her ivy dress.

"According to our books, the estimated gross profit should be tremendous unless the fleet ran into trouble." Marigold's purple eyes welled up. "Forgive me, Lady Sable, but I can't stop thinking about what happened. Your brother did Starkton well, and I respected him for that."

Sable cried. "Thank you. Abelot will be forlorn when he hears the news. Any updates on it?"

"The aggressors are speculated to be connected to the invaders from over two months ago despite the only main connection being the involvement of trade-related transportation. They could've been targeting the king and whoever else, but only got Richard and a few guards."

Struggling to regain composure, Sable stared outside. Under a maroon eave a fur-clad alchemist sold potions and herbs from their large table covered with herbs, mortar-and-pestles, alembics, retorts, potions, and empty bottles while a jester in green and purple motley danced and performed tricks. Rich and poor alike gathered 'round for the products and services. Sable squinted. "Why do Starkton's common folk choose poverty and slavery over riches and freedom?"

"I beg your pardon, Lady Sable?"

"They're uninspired, malnourished, and wear tatters after willingly restricting their precious mortality for someone else while their self-employed and governmental counterparts look like they just finished dining with the High King!"

Marigold's face reddened. "Some of those people are customers of your inherited ventures who can easily get their needs and wants fulfilled by your competitors, so please consider humility."

"Listen closely to my brutal truth. If you look outside with me, you'd be able to easily tell who works mindlessly for an employer's table scraps and who gets fairly paid by the masses. Richard worked forthright pursuing entrepreneurial success, and eventually gained the ability to hire employees, freeing his time while he ascended toward royalty. With all the ventures I inherited, I think I will enjoy my new life."

"Even though I manage Starkton Trade Company and the rental properties for you and Abelot, the businesses' progress is ultimately your responsib-"

The lighthouse's large brass bell rang, and then the others around Starkton joined its deafening chorus as a crowd congregated at the harbor. The ladies looked toward the lighthouse. *Silver Hare* and the fleet approached. "They're home! They're home!" many chanted as Sable Wyvern rushed to the berths and slipped. When she arose in her wet dress, an oaken carriage drawn by a white mare and filly loomed. "King Gwayne's already here?!" Sable wondered aloud as she approached *Silver Hare*'s lowering ramp.

Tyrian's black coat and Abelot's beard were unkempt, more so than the wrapped object reeking of rotting death in Abelot's right hand and book in the left. As the men approached their siblings, the crowd gave solemn silence. "Greetings," Abelot greeted with a smile.

Sable cried as she hugged Abelot tight. "A week ago there was an attack on the castle. Richard died defending himself."

King Gwayne's face was funereal. "I am sorry for your loss."

"Wh-wh-who did it?" Abelot asked with a cracking voice.

"They're all dead now."

Abelot's face tensed as he glanced away before asking "who i-i-i-ss th-th-th-the new Tr-reasurer?"

"High King Lesirion Strigil in the gold and ivory city of Honet sent Mace Doran of Honet Bank to act as Starkton's new Treasurer."

Tyrian took the object from Abelot. "A Doran?! I guess Mace will hate us once he sees this Doran head." He gave the head to King Gwayne, the crowd reveling. "She was Carillon Doran, Queen of Pylon."

Abelot held up his book. "If y-you don't mind, Your Grace, I-I need t-t…to get used to working with my-my new techniques, away from th-th…this large crowd and-and I'm unbathed."

King Gwayne put a hand on Abelot's shoulder. "Not yet. You're riding with me to the castle so I can properly bestow you the property Richard willed to you. Your sister already received hers."

GREATNESS

Starkton's snowfall has long since ceased, yet the air still chilled and untraversed ground retained defrosting slush. *Clip Clap Clop Clup. Clip Clap Clop Clup. Clip Clap Clop Clup.* But the weather didn't stop General Randall Bilteen from riding towards Abelot's smithy wearing his new fox head helmet, golden gorget, gauntlets resembling clawed paws and fox head shoulder pauldrons. Even Randall's silver stallion was helmeted with a fox head chanfron and House Bilteen caparison. When Randall almost reached the smithy, his steed dropped steaming dung in the road and an oblivious passerby stepped into it.

Bing! Bing! Bing! A ponytailed Abelot hammered blistering orange-red steel atop the smithy's anvil as his new gold and saffron-swirled armor with a matching dragon head helmet rested in the elongated workspace's back corner next to Morning Glory.

"Greetings, Abelot" Randall bellowed.

The ivory dragon centered on Abelot's breastplate returned the greeting.

"Your avoidance of mediocrity in every endeavor you've pursued reflects within your craftsmanship. I've recommended your work to Rickard and Robert, so expect a visit soon." Randall handed Abelot a sealed envelope and large pouch of gold. "In the meantime, here are the measurements of King Gwayne's royal guards and your compensation." Randall smiled. "The king should consider naming you Starkton's first Blacksmithing Master."

"Th-thank you, but I'm not g-g-g-g...giving up my sword f-for p-p-politics."

Randall then rode towards Sable and Marigold's nearby angelic harp and lute orchestra surrounded by an immense crowd tossing them money while draining bottles and flagons. Despite their performance, the symphony was disrupted by a drunkard in the crowd retching and...

"Thief! Give me back my gold!" a bottle-wielding drunk yelled at someone.

The suspect spat "You gave it to the bards, dimwit" just before the accuser broke their bottle over them, vaulting glass shards everywhere while they swung and swooped, chaos erupted, and barefoot patrons got their soles sliced open. Randall jumped off his horse and rushed to the fight, envisioning a potential riot while shoving people aside.

A King's Wisdom

When General Bilteen reached the aggressor, they clumsily slashed at Randall but missed as Randall retreated and unsheathed his falchion. "Drop your weapon!" he commanded when the alcoholic rushed forward only to slip and fall face first into the vomit left earlier, vomit and glass smearing into their clothes while they acquired numerous cuts. As the drunk rolled onto their back and got more gashes, Randall pressed the tip of his sword under the drunk's chin.

"Don't even think about getting back up. Guards! Arrest this one!" Some city guards restrained the aggressor as all stood before the general. "I hereby charge you with assault and battery with a weapon, attempted murder with a deadly weapon, and endangering the public with weaponry. You will be escorted to the dungeon unt-"

Huaahh! They vomited, and almost everyone backed further away.

"You will be escorted to the dungeon until further notice." The guards restraining the criminal took them away. Randall turned to the onlookers and commanded, "Everyone in this crowd, surrender your bottles and weaponry, then leave." As the audience complied, he looked to Sable and Marigold staring in shock. "Ladies, I apologize for ending your magnificent performance early, but public safety is of utmost importance. You need to hire more security for your next performance." As the audience departed, the musicians gathered their earnings while Abelot approached Randall.

"Excellent work."

"Thank you." General Bilteen climbed back onto his stallion and resumed patrol while Abelot returned to blacksmithing. Three hours passed before Randall returned to Abelot's smithy as he was securing it. He looked to the saffron sun within the heaven of wine, mulberry, and gold. "What's for dinner this evening?"

"The Prancing Fox."

"Good choice. Same for me."

They then proceeded to dine together at the Prancing Fox, Randall ordering chicken and dumplings with water whereas Abelot ordered their signature amber ale, cottage pie topped with mashed potatoes, and apples on the side.

MERCURY

Grace needs freedom from the tyranny of her charcoal burner's clothes," a fourteen year-old Múto whispered as the starred obsidian sky camouflaged him behind forestry and charcoal kilns near a river, smiling at a russet-curled teenager as she ate a honey-dipped pear, drank negus, and enjoyed festivities. He turned to the silhouettes of two teenage boys and a middle-age man hiding with him. "Any of you got any ideas?"

The man slid closer to the boys, his tan skin and shaved head reflecting the festival lighting. His icy pale eyes, fixed on Grace, sparkled as he licked his silver moustache and accented "Woo her with dancing like we Tavukish do…" He thumbed a dark book within his satchel. "…lest ye require magic in lieu."

I almost regret befriending this self-proclaimed 'wizard' over sweets. Múto hissed "That's horse crap, Koli." and slapped the back of Koli's head. The other boys quietly howled.

"You little…!" Koli paused. "It'll be easier with the distraction of Lesirion Strigil's coronation as High King in the Heart district's Marble Fortress once the scheduled performance of 'Nocturnal Lovers' Serenade' begins its three mile span." Drums rattled and stringed instruments thrummed. "I think it's about to begin." Bards across the metropolis fingered their strings and banged their drums in unison as sopranos, altos, and baritones sang "Nocturnal Lovers' Serenade":

> *Moon: Oh my subjects, showing loyalty*
> *The high and low, serving faithfully*
> *I bestow my light, so you can see*
> *The facade of my majesty!*
>
> *Night: Oh Queen Luna, how I relish thee*
> *Gracing my dark sky, so Earth can see*
> *Watch my children gambol with harmony*
> *You love me, unlike summer's sun rejecting!*
>
> *Moon: My strong noble Night, carrying me*
> *It's my honor to be governor of your hierarchy*
> *Even all your stars bow to me*
> *See the abundance my reign provides thee!*

A King's Wisdom

Both Moon and Night: Wise owls fly so beautifully
Ocean tides wave tranquilly
Stars surround us with jealousy
Let our nocturnal tryst be never ending.

Múto blushed at Grace listening to a bard's new song. "Koli, still no idea how we could pick her up? What about you, Uriel and Trystan?" The teens shook their heads, and one stepped forward to reveal his red hair, freckles, and blue eyes.

Koli pulled out his dark book. "You didn't take me serious. You wimps can't even ask a girl out, so I guess I'… we'll just have to use magic to get what we want."

What?! Múto wondered to himself as he and the ginger's eyes widened to the point where vision blurred.

The ginger piped "Impossible. What makes you believe this superstitious nonsense will work?"

Koli's eyes sparkled with his crooked yellow smile. "Trust this 'superstitious nonsense,' little wizard."

The ginger asked "Could you make my freckles disappear along with Trystan's stupid peach fuzz moustache?"

Trystan, still hiding within the darkest shadow, punched Uriel. "Up yours, ginger." Trystan stepped forward and taunted with exposed tongue. "I'm more of a man than you, shrimp."

Koli laughed. "Your childish request may be possible, Uriel, but I have to ask you all a question first. Can any of you read whatsoever?" They all shook their heads. "Well, I guess I will have to do the reading myself."

Koli opened the tome and placed it on the ground for the boys to examine. "The first spell we're going to use is simply called *Dance*, and is self-explanatory." He reached into his satchel and removed a miniscule amethyst. "But first, you need to hold one of these stones because of its properties aligning with the mind's potential energies. It's not abundant in Lantheon unless it's being closely guarded." Koli handed the stone to Uriel. "You first, do as I say. Extend your hand towards where you want to cast your spell, and say..." Koli deciphered the spell incantation. "Exulsimia, o, Exulsimia, o."

Uriel piped "this sounds like nonsense, but I will try it. Oxalemia, o, Exulimio." The bard's music became more upbeat. "What did I do wrong?"

Múto chimed "You didn't say the spell right." just before he snatched the amethyst from Uriel, pointed it at Grace and focused his breathing and attention. In confidence and initiative towards perfection, he chanted "Exulsimia, o, Exulsimia, o" and Grace started dancing to the music. Koli again bore his crooked yellow smile, but the boys were skeptical of Múto's gift.

"Boys, it seems Múto knows to listen when the wise speak and has dormant potential for magic!" Koli exclaimed in pride. "If he keeps this up, then *he* might be the one bedding Grace tonight."

Trystan blurted "Oh, this is awesome! What's the next spell going to be, 'cappy-tan?' Warming her up with my tongue?!"

A King's Wisdom

Koli's icy eyes sparkled at juggling torches near the bard performing to Grace. "Yes, you'll set aflame that bard's lute with *Fire.*" Múto complied, passing Trystan the stone. "You already know what to do…" Koli searched the book. "Igniblaz Fornax."

Trystan applied Múto's exact procedure for *Dance.* "Igniblaz Fornax." Following the incantation, one of the juggler's torches hit the lute, its heat warming the group from where they loitered. "I did it! I can use spells too!"

Koli's smile grew toward his ears. "I guess Múto is no longer the only new initiate." He removed a coin from his pocket, flipped it through the air, caught and examined it. "Múto, use the *Aphrodisiac* spell while we three try to charm the charcoal burner. It's 'Mitnudimagnes,' dweeb." Despite Koli's insults, Múto stayed with the spell tome while his associates approached Grace.

Sundering rage brought sharp pain across Múto's body alongside fire in his soul. *After everything I did for us, how dare you ingrates toss me aside like chicken bones and yellowed kale.* Salty tears singed his hazel eyes as he blurrily gazed upon his former friends join Grace in the festivities. *Is disrespect really my reward for listening to others?* Múto clung tightly to his one last friend. *No more! I will not tolerate this insult.* Múto glared upon Grace just as he growled "Igniblaz Fornax."

Fwoosh! Flames engulfed Grace and blanketed the wannabe swains sprinting to the river despite the juggler's painstaking control of their airborne torches. *"Find a bucket!"* the juggler repeatedly screeched amidst Grace's bloodcurdling screams and the whistles of her blackening flesh. *You will only fail,* Múto replied within thought as he dipped the spell tome and amethyst into the river where his friends-turned-bullies drowned themselves. *What have I done? Can I tell her goodbye?*

When he gazed upon Grace, her charcoaled mouth whispered "murderer, predator, sinner."

For the thousandth time, I am not the wretch you think I am.

Múto awoke to the stench and dampness of his wet bed. *The juggler swung when it should have been me*, Múto regretted as the Fropilé Verídom's bells announced dawn. "But I am now Brother Anton, a Verídom monk reborn three months ago from the ashes of a pirate who died at sea." he whispered before inserting his wooden dentures gifted by a local carpenter. He stared into nothingness with ocean eyes and a curling nose. *I am thankful for Bishop Wymund's incentive for me to continue my literacy studies and keep my dignity*, he thought while exiting the dormitory.

During his morning descent to the monastery's garden, warm-colored and ivory designs upon the walls balanced intricate stained windows. Upon reaching a saltwater pool surrounded by peach trees, two elder monks were praying in the bath. "Life has peachiness when it's searched for. Am I right, Salutis and Horto?"

"Indeed it does." one chirped through his white beard. He watched the pirate-turned-monk wince at the scar as he undressed, leaned to him and whispered "You shall grow with the amethyst in due time."

Are you kidding me? "That's why the bulge is still there?"

Salutis examined their surroundings, Horto staring to the sky, and whispered "Do you know why?"

"Yes." *I'd rather not.*

Horto's face brightened with his gummed grin. "Do y'all feel that?"

Salutis rose from the water and proclaimed "This is prime time to pray, and He answers sooner or later. Brother Anton, lead us in devotion."

Múto complied aloud, "Dear Verítamor, please bless us with overseas mission work." *To visit He-Who-Left-Me-To-Die perhaps?* "Amen."

Screams beyond the garden walls drowned the peaceful ambiance as the monks rushed to the garden's balustrade and bore witness a fleet flying House Doran's flag.

THE GOD OF
EMPTINESS

Girl, we all know I love sweet reds almost as much as my redheaded wife, but I have had my fill for now."

King Gwayne placed his meaty hand over his golden goblet. She acknowledged, pulled back the silver wine pitcher, and left it on the White-Grey Keep's mess hall table beside an unsealed document as she left the men to appreciate the hearth fire's crackling, warmth, and dancing. "How is it, Treasurer?"

Mace did not hesitate slicing off another piece of the porcini and citrus venison with caramelized onions and mushrooms on his plate, or guzzling the tart riesling. He met the flames dancing in the king's mismatched eyes. "A splendid meal, Your Grace. Thank you for the opportunity." He finished his wine. "But I assume you did not call me here just for dine and wine. Speaking of wine, is there a reason you've been partaking Starkton's lately instead of your usual Iytaleesh?" He gazed upon the pitcher. "And drinking less?"

"Starkton reds are cheaper than Iytaleesh reds… and I listened to Richard that fateful day when he counseled correcting my ways." King Gwayne picked up the document. "He was loyal, and the life-changing wisdom he bestowed upon me was not in vain, for he helped save me from myself."

"I barely knew him, yet knew his predecessors." *Abelot's a turbulent threat, just like Leggeron.* "Yet was at his side when his blood soaked the snow, a blessing and curse neither of his siblings got." *My gift from Alysse.*

King Gwayne held up his palm. "Let's stop dwelling upon the known, but upon the unknown." He laid his hand back down. "What do you think Richard contemplated, or possibly saw, as he was leaving this world?"

His successor, you ignoramus. "I've heard firsthand claims of lives flashing in an instant; for others, the best moment of their life; and even ascension to the heavens and descent to the underworld with born witness the deities and demons of lore. But my assumption is Lord Wyvern reflected upon all the choices he did and didn't make."

"When my time comes, I hope I relive the moment I started putting effort into living a worthy life." King Gwayne opened the document. "I called you here to share part of Lord Wyvern's vision for success."

"Thank you, Your Grace."

"I'm omitting the introduction and conclusion… *If you stay true to these principles, then you will move closer towards wealth:*

Saving: Save at least one-fifth, rounded up to the nearest well-rounded hundredth, of all incomes received, and either split it evenly between expansion and reserves or put the money entirely into reserves. Saving becomes much easier if arranged to occur automatically.

Expenses: Reduce expenses wherever possible, and seek equilibrium between quality of life and quantity of resources while living within your finances.

Skills and Education: Be always sharpening your skillset, pursuing mastery of few instead of mediocrity at many. Continuously train your mind like warriors in sparring grounds.

Income: Passive incomes build wealth when working alongside active incomes. Passive income can be acquired through numerous methods including business ownership, rent collection, and writing books and plays.

Risk Management: Mitigate risks by spreading resources instead of leaving them bundled, for catastrophes can happen.

Mentorship: A credible mentor is a partner whose guidance and insight can unlock potential.

Debt: Debt is money owed, not necessarily unavailable; and can be used as leverage for income production. The three acceptable debts are student loans, mortgages, and business loans. Cosigning debt is utter folly, for all cosigners can be penalized. There are two methods for effective amortization: Eliminate debt faster by stacking payments after some debts are paid in full, or save those untethered funds.

Self-Employment: Entrepreneurship is naturally much more profitable than a job due to customers directly paying for value whereas employees receive a small, usually capped fraction of an employer's profit. Dependent upon the situation, one's schedule can be freed by accomplishing tremendous labor upfront or hiring employees to do the work; or it can require many hours with tedious labor.

Quality: Quality determines whether one can attract opulence and warranted attention, or poverty and unwarranted alienation""

King Gwayne closed the document. "That's all."

"I expected a book-long letter, like the treatise a diplomatic emissary wrote to their prince. Did Lord Wyvern leave anything to split between Abelot and Sable besides ownership in Alysse's brothel?"

"He gave his will, but its legacy and bequest are between me and House Wyvern. I'm sure they'd rather have their brother with them right now instead of worldly possessions and money. Money is nothing more than a tool for those who know how to manage it, yet it serves as the god of emptiness for those who let it manage them."

That one sentence was probably the smartest thing I've ever heard this buffoon say except reading what Richard wrote. "Well spoken. Is this all you wanted to speak with me about, Your Grace?"

"Pour yourself more wine." Mace warily obeyed the king's command and spilled the sweet red on the table. "I should have addressed this long before now, but I postponed this matter since I didn't want to worsen your stress level as you've been settling into your new role. Are you kin to Queen Carillon Doran of Pylon?"

"Carillon is my sister, Your Grace."

"Do you still bear claim to Pylon's court?"

Sometimes I wish I kept that claim instead of building my own. "No, Your Grace, for I wanted to craft my own destiny instead of harming myself to fit into a mold unlike my brother Davirius who, due to Elysium province tradition, was preceded by birth instead of sex."

"Thank you for your honesty and loyalty. Before you came to town, Starkton was attacked months ago by invaders traced back to Tavuk and Pylon."

"I know of the attack, but is the connection to Pylon the beginning of a joke, Your Grace?"

"My brother, Starkton's Naval Master, sailed to Tavuk with Abelot Wyvern to address Emperor Septimius Ventneir regarding the incident. When they confronted the emperor with the evidence, your sister was with him and was ordered arrest."

Mace's goblet shook in his hand. "When is her trial?" he asked before sipping and spilling more wine onto the table and himself.

"The execution was fulfilled by Abelot after she ordered her guards to attack when she was charged after the evidence was presented. I have her head stored in a box so you could give her a proper funeral."

"I fought alongside that ungrateful bastard's brother when the White-Grey Keep was attacked, and he repaid me by killing my sister?!" Mace's face blackened as tears wetted his cheeks.

"The confrontation was before the castle attack which happened while you were here, and Abelot is blameless due to following orders and doing what was needed. But for clarity, I do not suspect your involvement since the catspaws tried to kill you, and I will not hold you responsible in your sister's stead since you've released claim to Pylon's throne and she faced justice." King Gwayne shook Mace Doran's hand. "You're free to go, and I'm sorry you had to learn of her death this way and this late."

Abelot will pay for her death one day, I promise with Dubuver as my witness. As an upset Mace Doran was leaving, a servant boy approached King Gwayne with letter in hand.

King Gwayne looked upon the boy. "Not now, boy. Bugger off."

"I have a message from Emperor Septimius of Tavuk." Mace stopped.

The king sighed and commanded "Give it here, and stay." The boy handed King Gwayne the letter, and he read it. "Boy, send for my brother and Sir Abelot immediately. My brother will probably be at the docks with his ship *Silver Hare* and Abelot is either at his smithy or today's tourney."

"Yes, Your Grace."

The boy left as King Gwayne poured himself more wine.

Sounds like Gwayne's getting what he deserves, Mace connived while keeping his back to the king, the fire comforting him, his mourns hiding a smile.

A TWO-EDGE SWORD

Four months passed since Abelot Wyvern executed Carillon Doran, yet his thirst for triumph never quenched.

Within the woodlands north of Starkton and southwest of Zenith Mountain, a full-armored Abelot and Bilteen brothers greeted countless attendees gathering to spectate Queen Alysse Sterling's chrysanthemum field tourney. *This crowd is much larger than last week's,* Abelot recollected.

Dum! Clang! Dum! Clang!

That luminous day, the Veritamor's Blessing chapel carillons resounded throughout Starkton's municipality as Abelot and a noble throng, surrounded by peasants, were escorted by zoomorphic-armored Sterling hares and Bilteen foxes to the chapel. *Clip Clap Clop*

Clup. Clip Clap Clop Clup. Alongside Abelot, General Randall Bilteen rode atop his steed while supervising the rooftop archers.

"Where a-a-are your brood?" Abelot asked.

"My generals-in-training are to be present in the armor you forged, Colette amongst the ladies, Marigold probably working with your sister."

Sable would not want to miss this, and I hope Richard's watching from the heavens. "And i-i-is it t-t-t-t...true High K-k-k-k-king Lesirion is c-c-coming? I-I don't know his sigil."

"I have neither witness nor intelligence of House Strigil's presence in the city, and his attendance is only a rumor." Randall eyed the congestion of peasantry. "But then again that may be part of the reason why this cesspool is hindering us." As the commoners near the colossal chapel began swarming the entourage and cheering Abelot, Randall commanded them to stay back while he unsheathed his falchion and his horse bucked. Sentries gained control of the crowd for the dignitaries entering Verítamor's Blessing's sanctuary.

Within the sanctuary, nobility lined every pew up to the altar lit by tapers in angel candelabras and imagery shone from stained glass windows, King Gwayne Sterling sitting in an oaken priest's chair between two moonstone cherub sculptures overlooking the altar. As Abelot and Randall approached the altar, King Gwayne stood and rapped his gavel, priests lit frankincense and myrrh, and solemn silence filled the room.

"Good people of Starkton, we are gathered here today for the anointed knighting of Abelot of House Wyvern, who has been recommended by fellow knights and your king. Are there objections?" Everyone remained silent. "This ceremony shall proceed. Abelot Wyvern, bestow thy sword, then kneel for the oath." Abelot obeyed, blinded by sunshine reflecting off his armor and Morning Glory, eyes watering as he met the cherubs' judgmental gaze and that of King Gwayne laying the sword's flat upon Abelot's shoulder. "Following my cue," King Gwayne commanded, "sing the knight's oath hymn 'Behold The Knight's Sword Oath.'" They then sang each line whilst the sword alternated shoulders with each verse:

Behold I: A noble cavalier so zealously bold,
Wielding sword so sharp, bright, and cold,
Armor shining as a lord's treasure of gold,
Protecting his lord's people, young and old.

Behold I: Shielding the law from vile tyranny of yore,
Defending the people from crimes brought by war,
Banishing oppressive fiends of this world, myth, and lore,
Delivering justice through the martial art of the sword.

Behold I: Swinging my sword firmer than a woodcutting axe,
Honing my mind, body, and soul before they go on their eternal racks,
Sharpening my skills in warfare and knighthood, never being lax,
Honoring myself and the public good through the consistent behavior I act.

Behold I: Upholding my integrity upright,

A King's Wisdom

Holding my sturdy shield upon my arm tight,
Carrying always my sword to keep peace, never to start a fight,
Keeping my promises in this knight's oath, for I am now a knight.

King Gwayne removed the sword and commanded, "Arise, Sir Abelot of House Wyvern, a knight of Starkton and the Lantheon Realm. May you never fail to bring the glory of morning unto the good citizens of Starkton." Abelot stood as the crowd cheered in the sanctuary.

And at today's tourney. Sir Abelot removed his dragonhead helmet and checked it. *I shall not fail to bring the glory of morning,* he promised in silence to the golden helmet's saffron swirls dancing in sunshine before reequipping the helmet.

Broo! BROO! A trumpet blared and herald cried, "First event, jousting! Event winner gets a horse leather jerkin, second place gets one hundred gold coins, and third gets fifty! Two out of three points determines bout winner. First bout, Sir Abelot Wyvern the Golden Dragon, versus Valus Vinearkh the Centaur!"

Abelot laughed, and everyone stared in confusion.

"Sir, are you well?" the herald asked.

"Wha-wha-what... What kind of d-d-d-d-dumb we-we-wench names th-th-their child a penis joke? Phallus!" Abelot continued laughing, and the crowd began to laugh with him.

Clup Clup Clup Clup! Clup Clup Clup Clup! Pisch!

Following rapid horse trotting, something struck the jousting fence, and Abelot's smile disappeared with the crowd's laughter.

"STUTTERING BASTARD!" Abelot turned to the snarled roar. Atop a spotted yellow destrier perched a burled, hunchback grotesque bearing no hair but a scraggly neck beard dangling below their deformed, scarred, yellow-eyed face. "How dare you mock the messenger of Greca's goddess of fertility and wine Cunnila when your grandfather Leggeron was also named after one of our gods!" Valus' tattered blood-red cape waved in the wind, its sewn wolf's head growling at Abelot. "I can't wait to smash your mockery and wear the jerkin."

How does this creature know of my grandfather and bastardy? I'll have to ask after I win our bout. "M-m-m-may the b-b-best m-m-m-m..." Alertness overtook Abelot. *What is this pressure emanating from the spectators?* He turned to the spectators; atop a log platform amidst them were Queen Alysse, the Bilteen sisters, and other nobles spectating alongside trumpeters and tournament officials. "...win, 'Valley.'" *Did I learn horsemanship fast enough last week to be prepared for jousting today?* Abelot wondered as Valus' face wrinkled when he was putting on his helmet before riding to his end of the jousting fence. After an attendant provided Valus a lance, Abelot rented a Grecan bronco from a horse trader, got into position and was handed his lance. Then the trumpet blared and Queen Alysse commanded the bout to begin.

The jousters raced towards each other with aimed lance. As they approached hitting range, Valus extended his arm toward Abelot's heart and knocked him off his horse.

"One point, Valus the Centaur."

Abelot scrambled to get back into position, and the contenders went through the same motions except Valus smashing Abelot just below his lance-bearing arm instead of his chest; Abelot fell.

"Two points, Valus the Centaur. Bout Winner!" The crowd cheered as Valus saluted and Abelot lied in defeat.

When Abelot crept up off the ground in humiliation, he felt the points of impact. His golden cuirass was dented. *I doubt this "Centaur" could beat me in swordplay.*

Valus trotted to him atop his destrier, lance still in hand. He eyed Abelot and the unmanned bronco. "Staying grounded suits you."

Get off your horse, and I'll prove you right; no, I mustn't, not here. "F-f-f-orgive me, V-v-v-v... Centaur." *Arrogance got the best of my ego.* "I now s-s-s-s-see wh-wh-wh-why y-you are c-c-called th..."

"Do yourself a favor, bastard dragon. What's that saying about hard work and talent?"

Now's my best chance to ask. "W-w-w..." Before Abelot could finish his sentence, Valus sped away, his blood-red cape flapping, its wolf's head growling and sneering at Abelot. *I need not further dwell on this failure or him; on to my strengths!* Abelot returned the borrowed equipment and refreshed before being ushered to knee-high chrysanthemums praising the majestic sun as Queen Alysse and a knight wearing a nine lavender-starred black surcoat awaited his arrival.

"Armed combat is about to begin." the queen decreed, her jade eyes glistening like antiquated copper shields when she beheld Abelot's broad shoulders. "Event winner gets a silver weapon of choice, second place gets one hundred gold coins, and third gets fifty! Two out of three points determines bout winner. For this bout, Sir Abelot Wyvern the Golden Dragon, versus Samantha Starlight, Sword Maiden of Dragon Fall! Contestants, salute and en garde."

When Abelot and Samantha removed their helmets and saluted, Abelot's heart fluttered into a million butterflies, simultaneous heartbeats filled his received audible soundwaves. Sun fire was Samantha's hair, midnight her eyes, divinity her face. The gateways to her beautiful soul reflected not the flower field but instead Abelot Wyvern holding his Morning Glory as she grinned so wide the corners of her eyes crinkled, and Abelot returned the gesture. *Why do I sense no adversity yet feel challenged?* Abelot wondered. *No woman has ever caused this. Are our souls communing?* Abelot withheld tears as they lowered their helmets to begin.

Then a servant boy ran to them, the Sword Maiden idled, and everyone except Alysse glared in scorn. "S…sir Abelot, I've been…," the boy gasped, "…searching for you." The boy gasped some more. "I went to ye smithy first."

Abelot growled "We need no interruptions, brat. Scram!" Samantha clapped.

The boy's rapid breathing continued. "King Gwayne sent me…I… gave… him a letter. He requests… he requests your presence in the keep." Queen Alysse could not hide her heedfulness.

The Sword Maiden removed her helmet. "Your Grace, can you please make him leave so we can fight? I would like to win my money already."

Alysse said nothing as she scowled at Samantha, strolled to the boy and squatted to his eye level. "Catch your breath, little turtledove." Alysse consoled. "I see the letter not in your hands, so he must still have it." She smirked. "Come with us to the castle, and we'll see the truth to your claim." Queen Alysse looked back at Samantha. "Abelot forfeits this bout in your favor, Sword Maiden, since he's coming with me and the boy in my carriage. Tell Lord Farquad and Lady Stella I said 'hello' when you return home."

ALPHA

O f course my brother's drinking the wine cellar dry." Tyrian remarked as he tapped the throne's silver hare armrest, its shine matching his grey streaks and tone. "We ought to be drinking with him."

Alysse scowled "Only the king, queen, and prince are allowed to sit upon Starkton's throne, Naval Master."

Tyrian squirmed on the sheepskin seating. "You'd exclude your king-husband's brother?"

Alysse's complexion darkened as she stamped her foot and screamed "THIS IS NOT THE TIME TO PLAY GAMES! I DON'T CARE WHETHER OR NOT YOU'RE HIS BROTHER, I COMMAND YOU TO GET UP OR GET HANGED!"

Abelot's hand crept to Morning Glory's hilt.

"Alright, alright." Tyrian mumbled while obeying the queen. "I tried to lighten the mood, Your Grace. I would rather still be on the beach watching the waves than waiting on my portly brother."

Agreed. Abelot nodded. "A-a-and I-I-I'd r-r-r...rather b-b-b-be at th-the t-t-tourney than here, m-m-my l-lord."

Mace's hazel eyes sparkled as he chewed mint leaves and chimed "I hate I missed the view, and tournament."

Tyrian smiled. "That's on you. Now I've waited long enough; I'm going to join him. Would y'all like to follow me, or bring you something upon my return?"

As the queen bore her teeth, Abelot held up his hand and breathed deep. "M-m-m... Maybe one g-g-glass t-to ease m-m-m-m-...my nerves, my lord."

Tyrian approached Abelot, looked him square in the eyes, and calmly placed a hand on his shoulder. "As you wish, Sir Knight, but enough of this 'my lord' talk for now. After everything you've done for Starkton, and vengeance we wrought in Fropilé, I..."

"I got a letter from Etauq Emperor Septimius Ventneir," King Gwayne roared while entering the throne room, gemstone goblet in trembling hand as he struggled to finish his drink. "House Doran is sieging Fropilé because of you two killing my Treasurer's queen-sister, so I suspect they're sending the rest of their offense this way. If left unchecked, they could conquer who knows what." Mace Doran smirked.

Chaos erupted in the throne room, and Abelot stiffened his body. "You-your Grace, she r-r-r-resisted arrest and-and-and had h-h-h-her guards try to k-k-k-kill us." Abelot glared to Mace. "If the-the Dor-r-rans ign-n-n…" *Curse this stutter!* Abelot smacked his thigh multiple times. "…nore that, th-th-then th-th-th-that's on th-th-them."

Mace's face darkened and eyebrows furrowed as he looked into Abelot's eyes and yelled "AFTER YOU KILLED MY BELOVED SISTER CARILLON AND I FOUGHT BESIDE YOUR BROTHER, YOU HAVE NO RIGHT TO-"

"SILENCE!" King Gwayne commanded as he slammed down his goblet, his green eye twitching to the bouncing gems.

Brief silence filled the throne room as Queen Alysse shivered before asking "How do you plan to answer this deadly riddle?"

King Gwayne closed his eyes, breathed deep, then gazed upon Mace. "Mace Doran, you may have abandoned Pylon's court and now serve as Starkton's Treasurer, but you're still of House Doran's royal blood, so you will stay as my hostage with all correspondence monitored until I deem otherwise."

With eyebrows still furrowed, Mace pulled back his shoulders and answered "Yes, Your Grace."

"Abelot, you will gather reinforcements while Starkton's military prepares. House Starlight of Dragon Fall, northwest of here within the heart of Lantheon's Three Seasons Forest, has a powerful army. I suggest starting there."

Abelot's eyes shone. *Lucky me! I wonder if that Starlight lady knight from the tournament will wine and dine at the Prancing Fox or another tavern before leaving town.* "Thank you, Your Grace."

King Gwayne looked upon Tyrian. "And you're sailing back to Fropilé."

Tyrian jumped back. "Wouldn't they expect imperial allies to attack?"

King Gwayne clenched a fist. "If you strike hard and fast enough, it'll be like fisting them with a square cactus and no olive oil. Make haste!"

"Yes, Your Grace."

King Gwayne turned to his audience and decreed "Our business has concluded. All may leave."

Just as Abelot stepped out into the courtyard, Queen Alysse grabbed Abelot's hand, biting her bottom lip. "Your Grace?" he asked.

Alysse clasped her dress at her thigh before she realized what she was doing. "Sir, I have something I forgot to give you." From her sleeve she removed a small gold necklace encrusted with tiny emeralds and amethysts carved into dragons. "For good luck, and me," Alysse purred as she donned it upon his neck. "Never remove it." She bore a toothed smile.

Abelot closed his eyes for fifteen seconds as he inhaled the aroma of the courtyard's bakery, listened to the steady circulation of the moat's watermills, and reopened them to serfs working. "Peace be with you, Your Grace."

"And with you be peace, Golden Dragon."

The queen gave her knight a salutary nod just before he trekked to Starkton's city limits.

When Abelot returned to Sable's and his stone manor to pack for the journey, he left his golden dragon head helmet on a table and styled his hair into a ponytail before heading into town ravenous and sore, his first stop being the Prancing Fox tavern near his smithy.

If this is my last meal at the Prancing Fox, then let it be my most memorable, he resented upon entry. Abelot then scanned the dining room. Amongst the customers congregating at the bar were the helmless Sword Maiden and Centaur sitting with sixteen gruff warriors being served from the bar by an hourglass-shaped woman. *It's now or never,* he concluded as he approached Samantha... until the worker called for him. They locked eyes and exchanged smiles.

"Good evening, Abelot Wyvern. I like your ponytail." She winked. "Ordering your usual, Abby?" The woman leaned forward, almost touching the countertop with her breasts. "*Or more?*" Abelot's penis hardened as he relived his previous experience between her legs.

"Th-th-th... Thank you, Maidron, but I'll b-b-b-be sticking with just m-m-m-m-...my usual cottage pie and amber ale..." Abelot grinned. "...and it's 'Sir Abby' to you, Queen of the Prancing Fox and She-Who-Puts-The-Bilteens-In-Their-Place-In-Here." Everyone nearby laughed... except for Samantha Starlight and Valus Vinearkh.

"I'm glad to see less stuttering and more confidence this evening. Did you have a good day at the tournament?"

Valus and Samantha sprang from their seat. Clenching her fists, Samantha screamed "HOW DARE YOU FAKE PRIDE AFTER

NEVER WINNING ONE BOUT!" and Abelot zipped into fighting stance, his eyes becoming iced flames of predation.

Brrraaaap! Everyone grew silent except for one patron who defecated in their breeches.

Maidron scowled "Take your crap out of my tavern." The person with the soiled pants sprinted out while the deformed cavalryman extended his middle finger to Maidron. "GET OUT! If you troublemakers don't leave, this Starkton knight *will* deliver justice! Abelot, your meal tonight is on the house."

Patrons cheered and cursed.

Bearing his spear onehanded, Valus snarled "A knight, a knight?!" Valus banged his fist against the horse leather jerkin he was wearing. "This quickly-unhorsed, stuttering disgrace is what Starkton considers a knight?!" He looked to the thugs around him, then to Abelot. "I never thought my predecessor's legacy would bear such an embarrassment. What are you really, Abelot Wyvern, just a blacksmith who plays with swords?"

So that's how you knew my grandfather. Are these guys your 'Latran Wolves?' Abelot smiled. "Yes, and wh-wh-what are you? Human, monster?" Valus grumbled and clenched his spear two-handed as Abelot eyed the brutes. "A fart in th-th-th-the w-w-wind?" The warriors grabbed their weapon hilts as Abelot then turned to Samantha. "And you should stick with-with knitting, lest y-y-...you prefer w-w-w-w-w-washing c-c-clothes."

Samantha screeched "You take me for a whore?! STEP ASIDE, CENTAUR, THEY'RE MINE!" as she charged toward Maidron.

During the Sword Maiden's charge, the Golden Dragon slid into her path, then side-stepped as his armored fist slammed into her cheek. *Thoo! Theh!* Whilst spitting teeth and blood, Samantha Starlight fell to her knees and Abelot Wyvern remained on guard.

"NAY!" Valus roared, snarled, and hissed. "Your sister will be pleasing me before you short me further."

The Centaur then looked to his accomplices and commanded their attack.

The Wolves charged, and the Golden Dragon smirked with stable breathing as its armored claws breezed the turbulence of stinging and slinging the prey. As Abelot's disrespect prevailed, Maidron shouted "Look out!" and goosebumps riddled his chilling skin while he dodged Samantha's sword swing.

Through the perked side of her lips, Samantha mumbled "You knogged muh teef ow!" and kept swinging, Abelot now answering with his bastard blade until he disarmed the Sword Maiden and kneed her in the face.

Falling onto her back with nose touching bruised cheek, Samantha went unconscious. *I wish our friendly competition earlier wasn't halted, but we now know who would have won, and I hope you forgive me and recover well.* Abelot wanted to comment as the Centaur rushed to her aid. Gnashing his teeth with glaring sapphire-flamed eyes, Abelot pointed his magnificent sword at the deformed mercenary. "M-must I sh-sh-sh-shave your n-n-n-n-n…neckbeard n-n-n-n-n-n-next, disgrace to Leggeron's legacy?" He then pointed towards the remaining defeated. "Or carve you to pieces?"

The sellswords lowered their weapons while Abelot's victory was cheered.

"If your blade wasn't sworn to Starkton's Crown, I would offer you a position within my band, just as your grandfather had many moons ago. Alas, your work is here and mine is to repair my client and escort her back to Dragon Fall."

"Wh-what a coincidence, the-the same place K-King Gwayne is s-s-s-sending m-m-me."

"We leave for Dragon Fall tomorrow morning."

Abelot eased his form. "Perfect. I can n-n-n-now enjoy m-my meal before sp-sp-spending the-the-the… night at Alysse's."

Maidron smiled then asked "Can I come?"

KNOCKED ARROW

*B*OOM! B*ADOOM!*

What good is going to come from this? Múto asked his newfound god in silence when he looked to the smoldering destruction of flaming boulders catapulted by friends-turned-enemy. Another boulder flew into a building, knocked a hole into it, and its inhabitants scurried out. *I wonder what bounty they bear!* Múto contemplated as a smile crept into the corners of his lips... before his chest ached as if struck by many grapplers. Brother Anton then shook his head. *Nay, I am not that wretched pirate anymore; the Lord provides my bounty.* the pirate-turned-monk acknowledged while turning his focus back to the Verídom's sanctuary.

"The Battlemage upholds us." Salutis led in chanting while he assisted medical workers, Horto portioned meals, and the elder Bishop Wymund supervised the relief effort...

Until the militant gaze of Bishop Wymund's pale cerulean eyes met Brother Anton's.

"Come hither." he commanded, a command Brother Anton obeyed with heightened alertness and without question. "True bounty reveals itself through selfless, focused purpose." The bishop pointed to a backdoor. "Gather-"

BOOM!

The building shook as rubble fell and everyone ducked before checking the damage. Bishop Wymund pointed to the door again and said "Gather donations onto the cart out back and haste thine return!"

Freedom for once?! "Yes sir!" Brother Anton bellowed with a brief nod before sprinting to the door. Once he opened it, Brother Anton found the wooden cart and his lungs were filled with brine and smoke. He closed his eyes and became Múto the pirate once again, grinning with a dancing heart as he rejoined his former friends. *No, I am not that man anymore*, Brother Anton reminded himself with reopened eyes and an anxious stomach focused to his new direction in life. *I am going until I'm done*; the pirate-turned-monk decided as he grabbed the cart's handles and began pulling it.

Creak! Creak! As Brother Anton passed many buildings, his cart's wooden wheels announced his presence to the hidden, and some donated to his cause. But he never let those small victories distract him from reaching the Ruby and Emerald Bazaar. *Is there anything left?* the lone monk wondered as the commercial center laid as ruins missing many of its namesake gems and goods…

…except for one untouched, gated shop.

The best rewards come from healthy challenges! Múto acknowledged in silence while remaining still and studying his surroundings. Lifeless; and upon this judgment, he then crept to the gate and peeked in. Behind the gate were veiled items.

Still studying the wares, Brother Anton paused and shook his head in shame. *There's only one way to find out if I found supplies for the relief effort.* Following a prayer for forgiveness, Múto grabbed a large piece of rubble and slammed it against the lock without progress, then continued failing until exhaustion. "This is worthless." the pirate-turned-monk proclaimed as he dropped the rubble and began walking back toward his cart.

However, as Brother Anton grabbed the cart's handles, a whistling flameless boulder flew in his direction. His body froze, shivering with rushing adrenaline, as the pirate-turned-monk's life flashed within his mind and he accepted his fate…

BA-DOOM!

…Until the boulder destroyed the shop's gate and roof, and Brother Anton stood unharmed. *Divine intervention again?!* The conflicted man rushed back to the shop, crawled over its mangled gate, and began excavation amidst lingering dust stinging his eyes and polluting his lungs.

While piling recovered blacksmithing tools and materials, the monk uncovered an onyx hilt sided with curved golden quillons and pulled it to reveal a dark crimson bastard sword lined with ultramarine V-shaped stripes separated by a deep cobalt fuller, invoking memories of all the pirate's impieties. He then swung his new sword and listened to its song, one he hadn't heard since his last day in piracy. "My service now includes defense," Brother Anton wheezed in awe. *Are other swords and armor amidst this rubble?* He searched the shop, examined his recoveries, eyed his cart…

…And wept.

"This is unacceptable!" Brother Anton wheezed in shame. He dropped the sword, but kept staring at it, the salvage, and his cart. *No, I know what to do;* Múto decided before finishing readying his delivery.

Upon the sweat-drenched, chaffed-leg Brother Anton's return to the Verídom, Bishop Wymund sat at an outdoor table covered with writing materials fidgeting a quill. "Unveil thine bounty." the bishop commanded as he rose and approached the cart.

Discuss only what's necessary and true. "I gathered food, bandages, water, tools-"

Bishop Wymund grabbed the sword strapped to Brother Anton's leg. "Unveil thine bounty."

Did he send someone to watch me?! Bowing his head in shame, the monk revealed the sword to his elder who then examined, sheathed, and returned it.

Bishop Wymund placed a finger beneath Brother Anton's chin and raised the monk's gaze to his. "Cahít Andíno's introspection unveiled his purpose for blacksmithing, which in turn begat this defensive and offensive tool. Had the god-fearing not been led to proper tools, then holy work would remain unfulfilled. Cahít bears no qualm against the holy, nor will ever."

Brother Anton trembled as he looked to the blazing sun while giving thanks.

Bishop Wymund then pointed to the supplies and commanded their placement beside a hall to the sanctuary's cellar door, which Brother Anton obeyed while never seeking assistance. Once finished, the exhausted monk stood near a stonewalled arch in that hallway watching the supplies get sorted and lounged against the wall to relax...

...Only for the wall to shake.

Someone needs to repoint these stones, Brother Anton acknowledged while looking to see if anyone noticed; none did. The wall then moved further back, but the stonework remained connected except swiveling on one side of the arch while the others opened into darkness. *Is this a secret passage, or just an empty space?!* Brother Anton snuck into the dark space, found a torch on a wall, cast *Fire* onto it and discovered an ancient mahogany door bearing a lock and hinges crafted similar to his sword. *Did the blacksmith who forged my sword also forge this metalwork?*

"He did." answered Bishop Wymund's voice from the secret passage's entrance. Brother Anton turned around and discovered the bishop blocking it. "However, who originally crafted this door remains unrecorded."

"Did you just hear my thoughts?" the monk asked.

A King's Wisdom

Bishop Wymund closed the stone door, approached Brother Anton, pulled out a keyring, selected a brass key and unlocked the door. "If ye will to know thine purpose and how life's trials hone you for it, enter. Otherwise, flee and forget this place. Choose."

Inquisition is far more valuable than ignorance. "Open it."

Bishop Wymund smiled. "So you walk with the wise instead of run with fools. Follow me, and mind thine step." When he opened the airtight door, luminescent amethyst walls with sharp cerulean ceiling crevices descended a spiraling burgundy staircase. Upon their entry, Bishop Wymund resealed the door and led the way.

Following Bishop Wymund's indolent descent, Brother Anton's aching legs wobbled and teetered towards sluggish crawling with occasional falls while the blinding light forced him to squint. After a while, a welcoming, indescribable holiness embraced the pirate-turned-monk while the walls began rotating and their purple light transitioned to pink.

"The changes indicate we're halfway there," Bishop Wymund noted as he grabbed Brother Anton's hand and placed it on his shoulder. "Keep yourself stabilized, and sing me a shanty to pass the time."

"This Mesireen shanty is called 'A Winebibber's Wish.' Pardon any butchery of its lyrics, I haven't sung or heard it since you found me." Thus the pirate-turned-monk sang as he and the bishop walked:

Honey, must you sail from our home,
Away from the grapes you have grown,

Bearing countless bottles warming bone,
Just for riches and your name known?

If you must go, let not vanity show,
For the jealous will see and know,
Wealth and progress may be in tow,
Inviting opposition to ample flow.

May fair weather bring you home,
Mead and riches abundantly flow,
Mirth ward Death's crow,
And Merriment fill where you go.

"That was much shorter than expected," Bishop Wymund grumbled as they stumbled upon an ancient cedar door. "But at least we're here. Welcome to the Esoteric Realm." Bishop Wymund then opened the airtight door to an open, crystallizing forest floored by large burgundy ribbons connecting the cedar door to platinum-doored trees guarded by sentries whose ears were long and pointed. "Those Elves are guarding gateway trees like the one I'm leading you to. But first, we will rest." After resting a few minutes, they approached a tree bearing a sign depicting a mind and book. "This is the Tree of Magic. Within is your next tutor. I look forward to collecting you when it is time."

As the bishop left, one of the Elven sentries opened the door, releasing a pleasant incensed fragrance wafting from a wood and crystal room covered with shelves growing from the tree.

Brother Anton entered the room and began walking to a bookshelf, but was interrupted by a female voice from a corner singing "Touch none but this one." He turned to the voice and found by burning incense and an onyx door a cloaked, tight-shirted elf whose ombré braided pigtails emphasized ears bearing two hooped diamond earrings, bloodshot lilac eyes and a perfect face. Using a smoking glass pipe swirled with warm colors, she pointed to an ancient book with ink and feather near her, and only when the pirate-turned-monk was near could the pipe's foul odor be smelled beneath the incense.

He dipped the feather into the inkwell and paused. "Must I sign my name from my past life, or the one I was given at initiation into monkhood? Also, I didn't catch your name when I walked in."

"Ramaya." She then studied Brother Anton's chest before remaking eye contact. "You bear strong magical potential. You must be the one Bishop Wymund told me about! Sign as Múto first, then as Brother Anton." As the pirate-turned-monk was writing, Ramaya leaned close and whispered "You must sign your old name due to your unpaid debt."

"To whom?!"

Ramaya directed him to the onyx door, it now glowing with indecipherable calligraphy. "Inside your individual experience, you'll find a book to study. Read it." She took a hit from her pipe and blew smoke at the pirate-turned-monk. "And enjoy the mirth." Ramaya whispered Elven tongue to open the door to a city at night, and Brother Anton passed within.

When Brother Anton turned around following entry, a tree stood in place of the door. *Where am I?* He stood near a canal just beyond the city's festivities. *Oh no, no, no! Where are they… we?! The spell book!* Brother Anton searched the area, found himself and former friends, pickpocketed Koli's spell book and fled into the city. *Did I just alter the past, or is this an illusion?* "It's time I pursue my destiny." Tears welled within his eyes. "What follows *Fire?*" the pirate-turned-monk asked himself with cracking voice as he opened the book to learn from his past.

The book's inside cover bore an uncolored sketch of a dragon grasping a pale horse within its claws.

SHORT & SWEET

I know deep down Sir Abelot is a great man at heart, Sword Maiden Samantha Starlight argued to herself for the umpteenth time as she watched the golden-armored knight snore beside her in the back of the wagon approaching the distant Three Seasons Forest surrounding Dragon Fall. *But will his warring duality ultimately sway toward righteousness or wickedness?* As a light breeze stung her broken nose corrected to perfection, she turned to an archer focused on the operability of his cedar bow, so focused he never noticed the wind's slight movement of his pointed huntsman's hat. "Apple-Eye…" she called to him.

Apple-Eye turned to her and twitched his grey moustache. As Samantha stared at the bridge of his nose separating one brown eye from a scar covered by a blood-red eyepatch, her mind was filled by a vision of him tied to a pole with an apple atop his head while an archer aimed to it.

"…thank you." she consoled.

Apple-Eye nodded and returned to work. *Thrum. Thoing. Thrum. Thoing.* Apple-Eye's rhythmic work sounded musical, and due to its harmony with the tranquil environment, Samantha became enervated, laid her head upon Abelot Wyvern's armored chest, and closed her eyes while basking in the smokiness of the brown-sugared bourbon steaks Abelot grilled last night.

Samantha reopened her eyes, now discovering herself surrounded by snow-covered trees circling a sapphire lake. "I'm finally home!" the sword maiden exclaimed wide-smiled and dancing featherweight… until only bird chirps broke the wintry silence over the barren lake, and finding herself in a purple dress with a dagger replacing her sword. *Is this a dream, or was my humiliation in Starkton a nightmare?* Birds chirped again, so she looked for them and found black-capped chickadees and scarlet cardinals feasting upon holly berries shading a bridge over a creek.

As Samantha walked to the bridge, grey blurs twirled amidst the other side; and once she stepped onto it, they became ravenous wolves. The sword maiden laughed, her laughter echoing across the battleground as her battle cry mocking this face of Death. "I need answers, so answer me!" she taunted unto the beasts.

One wolf rushed her while the pack watched the sword maiden easily toss it into the creek below. When the dishonored wolf was climbing back to the bridge, an orange one with stunted legs rose from the creek, countered it, and faced the grey pack with back turned to Samantha in comradery.

"Thank you," the sword maiden composed. "You are goodhearted."

DEVOTION

I could do this all day," Brother Anton bragged to himself as he reclined in a cushioned seat in a suite overlooking the Marble Fortress' auditorium. "Alas, I have work and studies which must be done." *But it can wait this time around.* "The bliss!"

"Did you hear that?!" an aristocrat exclaimed to his wife as he searched the enclosed area and never noticed the monk sitting behind them.

"No, honey," she responded.

"Good," Brother Anton whispered in her ear just as the curtains parted to reveal a seated orchestra dressed in finery behind an ivory-curled maestro bowing and waving to the audience. The maestro turned to the orchestra, hand gesturing to the violinists who started fretting and sliding their bow across the strings to carve brooks in a forest, then to the flutists with birds flying through the forest, and to the bass players whose herd of elk traversed the forest to the brooks. *How many times did they practice striving for perfection?* The monk gazed upon the book placed in the seat next to him. *How many times have I?*

This simulation within the Esoteric Realm repeated in perpetuity all aspects of High King Lesirion Strigil's coronation day, but Brother Anton's interactivity did not. When the pirate-turned-monk was not practicing and learning spells, the fruits of jubilation were consumed post-labor, but never before.

"Brother Anton," a feminine voice called from the suite's door. He turned to the door where Ramaya stood. "You have been granted ample time, yet I find you far from your expected station." She opened the door, revealing it now opening not into a hallway of the Marble Fortress but to the river near where Múto incinerated Grace alive. "Come."

They stepped through the door to the river, Ramaya closing it behind them, the door becoming a tree. Time slowed as the young Múto was about to light Grace aflame for the umpteenth time. Ramaya pointed to the doomed lady, and Brother Anton cast *Fire* upon her as tears rolled down his cheeks and he shook in guilt. "The ink on this page remains dry," Ramaya sang in tune with the music restored to full speed with time. "But your story does not." She retransformed the tree into the door, now leading to her space within the Tree of Magic. They entered and closed the door behind them.

Brother Anton checked the door's accessibility. It was sealed. "You need not dwell in the past, Pirate-Turned-Monk," Ramaya chided. "Only focus upon improving your current circumstances while minding the future." She grabbed a cloth sack from a table and opened it. Inside were odorous curled, dried herbs with green and white leaves riddled with crystals. "You now behold cannabis, an herb which catalyzes egregore to the Esoteric Realm when consumed in moderation with honorable intent."

Ramaya then presented Brother Anton a blue glass pipe covered with crimson and violet swirls, separated seeds and stems from a cannabis nugget, inserted its leaves into the pipe and gave the loaded pipe to the monk. He whispered *Fire* onto the cannabis and inhaled its grape-flavored smoke, entering euphoria as his body relaxed and mind transcended time and united with the universe. Ramaya's nose twitched. "Remember to consume this herb for spiritual enlightenment, to alleviate pain, and after accomplishments achieved through consistency, lest you descend the path to temptation's ruin." The monk's stomach growled and mouth dried as his heart raced. "And be wary of the side effects."

Brother Anton rushed to a small indoor pond and drank the best water ever tasted. Once he finished, the pirate-turned-monk stared at the stilling water growing flowers bearing oceanic blue petals and yellow bulbs with tips transitioning to the color of the petals. His hair and beard were whitened. "How long have I been here?"

"Long enough. Fear not the whiteness of your hair, for it is earned. Your consistent learning in monkhood earned you the opportunity to deepen your understanding. Congratulations on maintaining discipline and proving our confidence in your capabilities." Ramaya grabbed the cloth sack with one hand, his hand in her other. "It's time for you to reunite with your brothers."

Ramaya walked the monk to the door and directed a guard to escort him to the Verídom's spiraling stairway, where he ascended upright and nauseated. As Brother Anton reached his earthen home's door and knocked, Bishop Wymund greeted from the other side.

"The siege has ended." Bishop Wymund informed with a smile. They began rejoining those in the sanctuary. "The revelry has never ceased since the emperor's announcement."

"I bet Davirius and Nolryk are upset."

"They're dead."

"You jest!"

"Nolryk's ship fell first when foreign reinforcements decimated the Doran fleet, and an incarcerated gladiator hurled a spear through King Davirius' heart just before a gorilla sundered him."

"Who governs Pylon now?"

"Marilyn Yor released her Lions to all corners of Pylon daily until all opposition was plucked root and stem. Those who chose her colors over death were spared."

Something I know all too well. The pirate-turned-monk felt his chest's scars. "Queen Yor shall be an effective leader."

"The maintained purge of maleficence becomes the fostering of sustenance in due time…" They reached the sanctuary where Salutis and Horto labored with better results than when Brother Anton entered the Esoteric Realm. "…something you three must accomplish." Bishop Wymund called Salutis and Horto to them.

"Many thanks for restoring order in the temple and growing thy skills; thine time to mission is nigh."

"To where must we go?" Salutis inquired.

Bishop Wymund studied their attention as he answered "The Lantheon Realm, more especially Starkton."

Horto leaned back, eyes widening with eyebrows raised. "Doesn't Starkton already follow Verítamor?!"

"Many have been led astray by her queen's brothel."

This is no coincidence, the pirate-turned-monk acknowledged. "When do we leave?"

"Tomorrow morning before sunrise. Your departure and fees have already been settled with the captain. Grab all provisions necessary before you depart." Bishop Wymund reached within the sack at his waist and gave three coin purses. "This is your allowance."

All three monks replied "Yes sir!" and left the sanctuary to bask in the sun's gracious luminescence. Brother Anton looked around. Construction workers repaired buildings hit by catapulted boulders as the people rejoiced in salvation and commerce. Saltwater, cinnamon, and oranges fragranced the busy streets as seagulls glided to the solar serpentine dragon swimming across the bay harboring *Silver Hare*. *This is my chance*, Múto realized. He felt the sword sheathed to his leg beneath his raiment…

…And someone grasping the pirate-turned-monk's shoulder. "You need anything?" He turned to Horto.

To make sure my sword is sharp. When Brother Anton saw the water again, the dragon was replaced by rippling sunlight. "Only the essentials." *This is my chance.* "I expected a fleet, not just a man o' war." *Silver Hare, of all ships.*

Salutis approached. "I wonder if we're getting cabins or staying below deck."

Brother Anton smiled. "If Tyrian Sterling believes in karma, then he will bless us with cabins."

Horto tilted his head. "You know the captain?"

Yes, he and the Golden Dragon left me for dead. "By reputation." the pirate-turned-monk answered.

"I hope the weather stays merry." Salutis commented.

Brother Anton squinted. "Always be prepared for turbulence." His stomach gave a soft growl as he started walking away. "I'll meet you back at the dorm."

"Agreed." the others responded before all parted ways.

Brother Anton's stomach growled again. He walked around the building corner and peeked over his shoulder. Neither of the monks followed him, so he continued into the city by the street he searched for supplies and maneuvered to the Ruby and Emerald Bazaar once again.

Pork smoke smoldered from within, leading Brother Anton to a small restaurant where bronzed chefs with their dark hair fashioned tight labored in its open kitchen. Plates bearing seven corn wrappings sat in a corner of the kitchen window above a sign stating:

Daily Specials: Tamales, Steak Torta, Birria.

What the uptight don't know won't hurt them, Brother Anton justified as he ordered a plate of tamales with watered wine and sat at a table in a shadowed corner watching the restaurant entrance. The monk unpacked the corn leaves and revealed baked dough; once bitten, it filled his mouth with dry-rubbed pork and cayenne pepper paste. Ignoring the spiciness releasing endorphins, Brother Anton ate the rest of his tamales and leaned back in his chair as he finished his wine and reflected.

"Verítamor blessed me today." The pirate-turned-monk caressed his concealed sword. *Sword, clothes, tome, cannabis, fellowship; what else am I missing?* He studied a warrior squeezing a lime and pouring red and green sauces over beef-filled tortillas before dipping them into a bowl of spiced soup across from their wife eating cheese-covered rice topped with peppers, shrimp, and diced beef and chicken. Brother Anton smiled. *Armor and food for the journey!*

The monk left the restaurant and stepped into the sunset. "Where is it?" he asked aloud, his hidden sword clanking with his brisk walk. Upon reaching his destitute destination, his heart sank. *There goes the armor idea lest I find another smithy.* He then came across an apothecary selling dried mushrooms, fruit, and meat; and bought for preparation. *Do I still have the time and money for chainmail?* As dusk crept into the sky, Brother Anton finished his purchases, returned to the monastery, packed his backpack and slept.

"Wake up," two voices urged with shoves and candlelight. Brother Anton opened his eyes. Horto and Salutis loomed above prepared to leave. "It's time."

Not one worry clouded the pirate-turned-monk's mind as he climbed from his dry bed, grabbed his supplies, and all three monks left for the docks in silence. Once they reached *Silver Hare*, Tyrian Sterling stood at the foot of the docking ramp as Fropilé's dockworkers and his sailors transported goods to and from the man o' war.

"Good morning," Tyrian greeted, squinting at Brother Anton. "Where're you three from?"

"Bishop Wymund from the monastery said he booked a trip with you."

Tyrian exclaimed "You said the magic words!" and stepped aside. "Welcome aboard."

During their board, a hand grabbed Brother Anton's shoulder. He stopped, looked back, and met eyes with Tyrian again. "Excuse me, but have we met?"

A hot flash heated Brother Anton and brightened his vision before "You don't know me" erupted from the racing monk. As he reached the monk's cabin within the hull, the pirate-turned-monk lied upon a net hammock, sweat falling to the boards below as he closed his eyes.

Abelot Wyvern carved his chest as if he were a boy struggling to draw stick pictures in sand while Tyrian and his crew watched before throwing him overboard to die. Grace lit aflame and-

"I am washed clean of sin." Brother Anton controlled his breathing and embraced the sting of his baptism's saltwater burning his eyes and extinguishing Múto's flames harming Grace. "I am at peace." When Múto looked away from Abelot Wyvern's callousness, gentle ocean waves bestowed ancient, holy knowledge for Brother

Anton to study in solitude. "I am a disciplined man." The revels of Múto's piracy were overshadowed by Brother Anton's mastery of the arcane.

"Brother, you good?" a familiar voice asked. Brother Anton opened his eyes, tension releasing throughout his body. They watched as Tyrian Sterling brought a fresh water pitcher and plate of black bread. The pirate-turned-monk turned to the window. A peach and magenta sunrise glowed across the Elysium Sea.

"I am good."

"Nay, you are great." Horto praised. "The bishop told us you can further our training in restoration."

"He knows?" While Brother Anton procured the spell tome from his backpack, the cannabis sack fell to the floor and spilled.

Tyrian studied him as he regathered the herbs. "What's that?"

Brother Anton gave him a nugget. "Smoke this herb at your convenience, more especially when you want deeper contemplation and relaxation." He turned to the others. "We will as part of the training."

Tyrian grabbed his chest. "Thanks, sounds like it'll be good for a problem I'm having. I'll grab a pipe from an apothecary before departure." Tyrian then left.

"What else lies behind the hidden door?" Salutis asked.

"When granted the opportunity, dive within." Brother Anton chimed and grinned.

Horto looked throughout the hull before pointing to the tome. "Tell us more about that."

"This ancient tome holds the key to creation and destruction." Brother Anton flipped through the book, studied a page, then unsheathed his hidden sword and sliced his finger. As blood dripped to the floor, he chanted "Sana Sui," while focusing upon the lesion. It sutured and disappeared. "This spell is called *Self-Healing.*"

Horto blurted "This is witchcraft! Heresy!" As Horto was mid-lunge to the book, Salutis grabbed Horto's fist and consoled him.

Brother Anton marked his place by enclosing the book upon his middle finger as his others held the front and back covers. "If it is heresy, then did Bishop Wymund command me to train you or not? Were my studies in solitude for nothing?"

Horto eased his temper and rejoined his brothers. "Did you bring more copies of this book?"

"I have only this one. If blank books with ink and feather can be acquired then the restoration teachings may be transcribed. Hopefully our memory will allow recitation needless of transcription."

"I'm ready to learn," the acolytes responded, and thus their studies in the arcane art of restoration and health began before *Silver Hare* set sail for Starkton. To break from education, they ascended atop deck, Brother Anton issueless and sometimes volunteering in shipmate duties whereas Horto struggled with seasickness. Staring ahead, Brother Anton commanded Horto to follow his example until it dissipated before descending to their cabin.

"I noticed something," Brother Anton mentioned one morning a week into their voyage, "and I wish I addressed this sooner. Within this holy art you each have strengths. Salutis, you have a knack for healing whereas you, Horto, excel in cooking and dietary needs. Make these your primary focus, but don't forget to st-"

Dun! Dun! Dun! Dun! Dun! Dun! Dun! Loud running creaked into the hull as someone yelled "SOMETHING'S WRONG WITH THE CAPTAIN! SOMEONE HELP!" Everyone below deck rushed to crowd around Tyrian Sterling's cabin. Brother Anton's heart raced with adrenaline coursing his veins as the monks were ushered within by a couple lieutenants who knew of their medical aptitudes. Burnt cannabis from a pipe on a table and feces fouled the cabin as Tyrian lied motionless upon his cot, right hand placed over his heart, lightless eyes watching nothing.

Salutis checked his pulse, his breathing, then declared him deceased. "Judging by the hand over his heart, and mentioning last week he had a health concern, the heart-testing properties of cannabis must have induced cardiac arrest or a heart attack. Brother Anton, is there any way to revive him?"

Brother Anton knelt above the dead captain and prayed in silence, everyone else following. When he finished, he examined the room and doorway. Nothing changed. As the pirate-turned-monk closed the eyes of a captain who once left him for dead, he declared, "It is Veritamor's will Tyrian Sterling parted from his earthly vessel in peace. We must prepare a funeral service, lest it be held in Starkton."

Divisive chatter across *Silver Hare* ensued until the first lieutenant commanded to Brother Anton "You're the wisest of the holy; it is your honor." The rest of the ship unified with the decision now encumbering the pirate-turned-monk.

Salutis asked "Downstairs, we have a spare barrel of honey, do we not?"

"Aye," a sailor responded.

"But there are plenty of House Sterling banners," another replied.

Brother Anton searched the room until he found Tyrian's eyepatch and cutlass. "With these items and the barrel of honey, we can have a ceremony at sea, and naval burial by King Gwayne at home."

The lieutenant declared the matter settled and gaveled the table with his fist. Thus the shipmates and monks brought a honey barrel to the deck and embalmed the body within, scraping back into the barrel honey pouring over its edges. Once finished, the barrel was carried to the mast and covered with a Sterling flag. Brother Anton then requested everyone gather on deck, the monks surrounding the body, they being surrounded by the shipmates based on rank as light rainfall dampened their clothes.

"Shipmates of the *Silver Hare*, we are gathered this moment to perform a naval funeral ceremony for Captain Tyrian Sterling preceding the formal funeral which will be held in Starkton. As Tyrian's body will be secured within the captain's cabin until his surviving king-brother and family send him on the eternal sail," he held up the eyepatch, cutlass, continued, "we will symbolically lay to rest his most prized vocational tools, one for vision, the other defense. Tyrian Sterling has no need for ambition, nor to defend himself and crew, for his transcendence to that holy, eternal voyage shall adieu. Let us pray." After monk and sailor alike knelt in prayer, they sang the hymn "Eternal Voyage" as the first lieutenant and Brother Anton carried the items wrapped in a Sterling banner, singing:

> *Lord, grant thy serenity unto me*
> *Smooth tide ebb to gold beach*
> *I lay my sword in peace*
> *So this soul can sail on your sea.*

> *Lord, grant thy guidance unto me*
> *Day and night, lighthouses see*
> *I wave thy banner flowing free*
> *So this eye can envision your golden sea.*

> *Lord, grant thy strength unto me*
> *Dolphins jump in glee*
> *I fulfill your will, as I should*
> *For your judgment and blessing are always for best good.*

After the hymn concluded, they laid Tyrian's wrapped eyepatch and cutlass into the ocean, carried his barrel-turned-casket into the captain's cabin and covered it with a Sterling banner for the remainder of the voyage to Starkton, the first lieutenant commanding *Silver Hare* until then.

Three weeks passed after Brother Anton's ceremony, and he now stood at the bow of *Silver Hare* watching as the man o' war sailed into Starkton's Titan Bay. "I never thought I'd see you again," Brother Anton greeted to the solar serpentine dragon swimming across Titan Bay.

"You talking to me?" a sailor called from behind.

Brother Anton turned to them and responded "It's been a while since I was last in the Lantheon Realm before monkhood. Say, how long have you been standing there?"

"Apologies, milord." the sailor said before walking away.

"I'm neither lord nor abbot." Brother Anton responded as he turned back to the dock. The dragon disappeared. The carillons of Verítamor's Blessing rang throughout the city. "Someone must have the answers I seek. But to whom do I ask?" As *Silver Hare* docked, Brother Anton gathered Salutis and Horto. "Do you two see that chapel? Unless Bishop Wymund or Captain Tyrian told you otherwise, that's where we need to go."

"You know Starkton?" Horto asked.

"Partially. Although we're an ocean away from the monastery, remember to avoid the brothels."

"Aren't you to come with us?" Salutis wondered.

"Someone has to help deliver the casket to the king."

The monks nodded and began their trek to the chapel, Brother Anton searching the wharf until he and the first lieutenant came across an office building with a sign stating "Starkton Trade Company." As they opened the wooden door, a silver-eyed woman with copper hair sat behind the shelved desk sorting paperwork.

"Good afternoon." she greeted while meeting their gaze. "What logistics needs do you need fulfilled?"

"My lady, we're here to register *Silver Hare* re-docking in the bay." the first lieutenant stated while handing the woman his paperwork. "And here is our bill of lading. We also have urgent business with the king."

"I'm surprised to see someone other than Tyrian visiting me, sir. You need to go through Trade Master Deevon Yor or preferably your captain for gainful audience with King Gwayne."

Brother Anton responded, "Milady, we bear grave tidings best left for the king to hear directly from *Silver Hare*. May we gain assistance from Master Yor?"

"Yes sir. Excuse me, sir, but what is your name?"

"Thank you. Brother Anton. And yours?"

"Sable Wyvern." She pointed to a purple-eyed, square-jawed blonde sitting at a table near the window eating a sandwich. "And Marigold Bilteen, at your service."

FLIES

Mouna's charcoal hair tickled her nape with each pumpkin-scented gust, always bringing a more pleasant experience than her chaffing helmet strap and marching several miles from Starkton with countless more ahead.

To weaken her pain, Mouna often dulled her vision and reminisced lounging with her husband in their straw hut, listening to their three sons and daughter prepare supper following Mouna's hunting trips and tending their livestock...

...but those days ended when she returned from a weeklong hunt to the village overran, her family missing. During investigation of the tragedy, the Latran Wolves mercenary company, under Leggeron the Stern's leadership, revealed they exterminated the suspected goblin culprits; deeming them worthy of fellowship, she joined the motley band.

Despite Mouna's preceding village huntswoman role, she wasn't allotted riding horseback in Valus Vinearkh's vanguard, but Apple-Eye rotated archers riding in his cart, and whether by chance or pecking order, Mouna got her cart ride when the large caravan reached the Three Seasons Forest's Autumnal Ring.

Pretending to study for opposition and game, Mouna watched the magic forest paint itself in ardent autumnal colors and an overhead hawk arrowing while her heartbeat and discreet bowstring plucks orchestrated a private serenade. *Would the Elves accept me into their fold, or forsake me for hunting game since childhood?* Mouna pondered upon her lifelong dream of dancing through trees, singing flowered music to animals, escaping mundanity with the Elves… even if the general populace recognized them as an extinct race.

As she continued the peaceful strum upon her makeshift yew lyre, a passenger shifted. Mouna glanced their way, smelling the aroma of apple pie still lingering on the Golden Dragon. *Is he really the grandson of my old captain?* The Sword Maiden napped beside him, head lain upon his armored chest. Mouna smiled. *I'm glad she's warmed up to him after their fight at the tavern.*

Mouna firmed her grip on her yew bow. *One of these days I'll find Donald, Mary, Gary, Joseph, and Henry, all happy and healthy.*

Mouna blinked and found herself cuddling with Donald against the autumnal breeze flowing beneath their favorite dogwood tree beside the sheep pen near her childhood home, a simple log cabin intended for pursuing peace and ignoring life's cruel cycle of comfort, descent, hardship, and ascent. Blunt pain in Mouna's left side forced her to blink again. She jumped as Apple-Eye pulled back his hand and stopped the cart amidst winter's engulfment.

"Please forgive this neglect, milord. It was an accident."

"Ye're on watch duty all night for this. We're here."

Dragon Fall, a dragon's skeletal hand hollowed and reconstructed into an impenetrable fortress with moonstone additions and decorated with House Strigil's owl banner, stood on a manmade island within the sapphire crater-turned-moat. Bards often sang of the legendary Battle of Dragon Fall, where the Three Seasons Forest's Elves perished against the Goblins just before Verítamor sent Dubuver's mortal vessel crashing into the heart of the Winter Ring.

Around Dragon Fall's moat were many tents erected within thick snow surrounded by siege weapons and House Starlight banners. A soldier passed Valus and approached the cart from the edge of the drawbridge closest to the forest, covering their face with a purple balaclava hanging around their neck. "Halt! Where are you from, and what business do you have here?"

Valus Vinearkh growled "Starkton."

The soldier stepped away. "A carrier hawk's message claims a foul pestilence has overrun the city. What business do you have here?"

Before Valus or Apple-Eye could respond, Samantha Starlight approached the front of the cart. "Lady Samantha of House Starlight returns home by escort of the Latran Wolves. We have been away from Starkton's city limits for some time now; when did the plague start? We have none sick we know of."

"Welcome home, Lady Samantha. The plague started not too long ago, most likely brought by foreigners."

"Then we're a lucky lot who departed before it began." She looked around and squint her eyes. "What's going on?"

"Shortly after your departure, Lady Stella attempted to overthrow Lord Farquad Strigil, only to get captured. We are besieging your home and trying to avoid damaging Dragon Fall or your mother, my lady."

"I left home expecting to face *enjoyable* challenges in Starkton's tournament, not return to hellish ones."

"Please forgive our shortcomings, my lady, but we believe one of Lord Farquad's men may have escaped. Farquad is cousin to High King Lesirion, and if we don't reach a diplomatic conclusion soon, either Lesirion's army or overexposure to the elements will end us all."

"I do my best to learn from the mistakes of others, and don't intend on repeating my mother's. Whether we starve Farquad into surrendering or paint Dragon Fall's walls with his blood, we will restore peace and rescue her." Samantha turned to Abelot. "Either way, he needs somewhere to rest until he can return home safely."

"As you command, my lady. However, what business does the famed Golden Dragon have here?"

Abelot knocked on cart railing. "My king th-th-thinks we will be inv-vaded by a foreign th-th--th…" Abelot smacked his thigh twice. "…threat soon and needs m-m-m-m-more soldiers."

"I see."

Apple-Eye turned to Abelot. "Don't forget about us."

Valus released a primal growl and snarled "Why was this undiscussed while we were still in Starkton?"

What a great idea! Mouna's face brightened. "It would be an honor to pro-"

Valus pointed his spear to Mouna. "Nobody asked you! Know your place."

"I need to repay m-"

Valus hissed "You disgraceful slag!" and blackened Mouna's left eye with his spear hilt.

Just as Valus lunged to grab Mouna's shirt, Apple-Eye nocked an arrow, aimed toward the infamous Centaur and rebutted "You're not going to unnecessarily strike any of my archers."

Abelot's brows furrowed. "I was too busy kicking Wolf ass to get the opportunity to facilitate your foulness meeting King Gwayne."

Mouna crept another smile. "Your stutter alleviates when you're grumpy."

Apple-Eye gave her arm a light bump. "Go hunt game and firewood."

"Yes sir." *Thank you for letting me return to familiar territory.* Mouna hopped over the cart's edge and landed in snow meeting her knees before starting for the woods. The snow only thickened to the trees as it continued descending from the clouded heavens, yet the forest's evergreen canopy kept the bed dry and traversable compared to the lakeshore. However, the same canopy which maintained dryness also darkened the forest.

After her eyes adjusted, Mouna gathered large branches and bound them with vines to craft a sled before building a one-person shelter, digging a fire pit and lighting it when dusk loomed with her waning vision and encumbering body. *Tomorrow is a new day, and I was sent alone*, Mouna realized as she had no choice but to refresh herself in destitution. Her lit flame's warm colors could not repel nocturnal darkness creeping behind her eyelids and into her dreamless slumber…

Before her eyelids sensed those colors return missing their heat.

"Ho! Ho! Ho!"

"Hee! Hee!"

Mouna's heart raced as she pissed her pants and reopened her eyes to her fire pit's dwindling embers. *The smoke and light must have brought them here; how stupid of me! Was the light I sensed my fire going out?!* Mouna contemplated as every violation imaginable riddled her mind while she readied to defend herself. She steadied her breathing, answered "show yourselves, prey of my hunt" with steaming breath…

And then froze.

Luminescent warm-colored apparitions danced all around and levitated above sword length, even dancing through the air like fireworks or spells forgotten long ago. One produced harmonic vocal noises; the others followed suit, each face smiling… and each ear long and pointed. *Are these things taunting me?* Mouna recomposed herself and aimed in shivers at the one who started the resonation.

"Oh ho!" the sprite giggled. "We greet you with song, you greet us with fright. Fear not, huntress Mouna, we desire naught you'd deny."

"What makes you believe Mouna's my name and you know what I seek?"

"Young acolyte," chimed the sprite with open arms, "don't you recognize us?" It wiggled its ears with a laugh in tune with the melody.

"The Three Seasons Forest's Elves died ages ago, so who are you?"

"Have we not made our spiritual ascension visible unto you?"

"You decided to appear unto a lone female?"

"Donald, Mary, Gary, Joseph, and Henry have been within your heart this whole time." It gave the shivering, steam-breathed Mouna a thorough examination head to toe. "Your warmth is much greater internally than externally." They extended their hand. "If you don't restart a fire or follow us, you will freeze to death."

Mouna lowered her bow, quivered her arrow and eyed her woodpile. "Which is faster?"

"Despite your outdoor survival skills, traversing with us should heat your body long enough to reach *your proper destination*."

"Lead on."

They all disappeared except for one whistling deeper within the still woods as Mouna followed. When she reached it, the sprite disappeared, another appeared elsewhere, and the process repeated. Her path warmed while snow dissipated when the seventh lit her way and miniscule moonlight bleeding through the treetops revealed foliage changing from dark and dreary to light and merry. *We're somewhere in the Autumnal Ring*, Mouna realized as she marched forth. *But where are these spirits taking me?*

"We're almost there!" the tenth sprite proclaimed.

Mouna stopped to rest her aching legs and hips on a fallen branch covered in vined rose-colored flowers hanging like moss. *These flowers almost blend with the autumnal colors.* She looked up and was sheltered by more. "What type of tree is this, and why did I not see any earlier today?"

"It is wisteria, growing away from the worn paths. You need to press onward." Mouna obeyed, popping her lower back after she rose. During her trek to the eleventh sprite, some trees had rubs and branches pruned, with massive hoof prints in sets of two marking the soil beneath, leading a different path.

Mouna's stomach pained from starving for several hours. *That beast could feed me and who knows how many other Wolves.* The huntress stared at the path of hoof prints and back to the whistling sprite. *The Wolves and my temporary state do not matter right now*, she decided before continuing her designated route. *Besides, I cannot see well enough to hunt until dawn.*

A King's Wisdom

Upon meeting the eleventh Elven sprite before two perfect rows of wisterias, Mouna stopped. "Excuse me-"

She looked over. The spirit was gone. Goosebumps riddled her arms. *This must be the place.* Mouna stood for a minute and glanced around one last time. There remained no sign of the Elves except for the natural path ahead. *I am the only person stopping myself.* She put one foot forward in caution, then her other, then committed to following the trees. Her senses heightened. Comfort embraced her touch and patchouli her smell, however silence held strongest this territory; not one nocturnal bird chirp could be heard past the trees, nor the Elven music or even her footsteps...

...Until wind passed through wisterias circling an open floral grove ending the path. It felt safe enough for Mouna to mark her trail with her helmet next to the grove's entrance. *Where did they go?* No trace was left, or threat detectable. Mouna's mind and body began to relax once again. *If I don't figure out where the Elves want me to go next, I'll rest here and resume my duties to the Latran Wolves in the morning.* Mouna closed her drooping eyes while struggling to stand upright. No Elven music played. *Is this silence deliberate?* She reopened her eyes to no change. Mouna started staggering along the grove's edge. "I give up."

"Don't," a voice whispered as if somehow within her mind.

"Where are you?" Mouna mumbled. The huntress blundered her footing and hit the ground, head smashing onto a rock. As her body remained in ecstasy despite the fall, the rock produced a warm liquid.

Mouna closed her eyes and rested in peace.

When Mouna awoke well-rested and unencumbered, the surrounding flowers became as luminous planets and stars painting their dusked woodland universe. Upon revisiting the path, Mouna beheld not her helmet but instead two cool-colored winged pixies levitating, one blowing through a grass blade as their musical instrument, the other holding a hollowed twig.

"We've been waiting." the twig-bearing pixy sang before orchestrating a celestial tune.

"Enter." the other charmed before harmonizing their grass blade.

"Who are you?" Mouna asked. She felt her clothes change, and found her mercenary armor was replaced with a silk gown.

"Salvation," *a voice whispered as if somehow within her mind.*

Mouna followed the path back to where the Elven sprite disappeared, walking on clover-spotted fescue instead of fallen foliage, surrounded not by silence and lifelessness but by celestial music and dancing pixies. As she revisited that place, the hoof print trail and marked trees were replaced by blueberry bushes growing outside hollowed trees emitting mirthful voices. "Have my dreams become reality?" Mouna asked, seeking response from familiar voices as she stepped into yellow light stretching outside a window of the merriest dwelling.

"Ho! Ho! Ho! Welcome to your proper destination!" greeted a grinning Elf in a kaleidoscopic robe sitting at a feast surrounded by Donald, Mary, Gary, Joseph, and Henry.

CANDLES

Starkton's lifeless ruled her land whereas their stench and pyre smoke controlled her ashen sky. Most still alive locked their doors, even at the White-Grey Keep and Verítamor's Blessing, lest masked sentries, clergy or doctors approached. But on Starkton Shipping Company's front porch, Sable Wyvern played her harp as a fevered, short-breathed General Randall Bilteen brooded near the porch's far edge, staring onto Titan Bay's emptiness in deep thought.

Jolenta, my lovely wife and Mother of Starkton, know during these trying days I dwell upon your birthing of our four pups, the Usurper's castle, and your raising of Her Grace's establishment from a small guildhall. But why favor the Usurper who started the twenty-year "Hop of the Rabbits" instead of Jon Lilan's legacy? He reached to his armored silver stallion's rein and clasped it. *Why choose your slow, agonizing death to ovary cancer and leave me to raise*

Robert, Rickard, Colette, and Marigold alone? I fail to understand your logic during what could be my final days, and am failing to win a war which cannot be won by sword. But beneath the stars I swear by all the gods that my victory will be an admiration the Lantheon Realm will know for countless ages, yet could never amount to the many of Starkton's Mother. As Randall climbed onto his warhorse tearless and stone-faced, Sable said her goodbyes and continued playing her silver harp with ocean eyes. The general coughed and nodded before riding away.

Clip Clap Clop Clup. Clip Clap Clop Clup. As Randall Bilteen traversed the dying city, priests prayed and soldiers worked to aid Starkton's recovery. He halted his steed upon reaching a writing military officer.

"Lieutenant…" Randall coughed without control. "…Dead today?"

"Ninety thus far, Sir."

If this rate keeps up, then the whole kingdom could be next, then the surrounding provinces soon after. "Soldiers?"

"Zero, Sir."

At least no sentries have succumbed to the Usurper's plague yet. "Has the origin of 'King Gwayne's Plague' been discovered?" Randall coughed again.

"Origin still unknown, Sir, but social isolation and close proximity to fire have been slowing its spread, Sir."

"Keep all fires lit and enforce isolation."

"Yes Sir."

"At ease."

The lieutenant returned to their labor as General Bilteen continued travelling to Alysse's Brothel. When he got to White Dragon Street, traversal within its silent peace felt as pleasing as sex… until his steed bucked upon reaching the destination. Once Randall Bilteen regained control, he dismounted to drag the frightened horse inside, but it froze and expelled all bodily secretions before submitting to Randall's command and grazing on the brothel's mint rushes upon entry.

Neither afflicted nor healthy lingered within the front lobby's mauve, elm-lined walls, only the scent of mint and a five-foot tall marble dragon statue in the center. "Where did the couple go?" Randall Bilteen asked aloud.

"Elsewhere." retorted a female voice from behind. Randall turned to the voice and discovered Queen Alysse wearing a gold and pearl necklace over her scarlet and violet priestess' dress, its skirt draping the floor. "And I have a blonde equestrian who'd love your stallion." Alysse winked.

Randall's blushing face matched his armor. "Your Grace…" Randall coughed without control.

Alysse's jade eyes sparkled as she purred "My girls are clean," which echoed and summoned a short-haired blonde, ginger, and the olive-skinned beauty Crystabella from nearby rooms, all symptomless of King Gwayne's Plague. She pointed her right index finger upward, and more stepped out of upstairs rooms, all also symptomless. Alysse then gave a seductive grin and walked in confidence to an intimate proximity and purred "And, I heard some foreign priests roaming

Starkton are healing those not too far gone." while tapping on Randall's cuirass.

Randall took three steps back then coughed again. "Your Grace, stay back or y-"

"I'm not scared of the plague."

Randall squinted as he continued coughing. *Those 'priests' could be the ones who brought this plague to Starkton, lest they are why no infected are on White Dragon Street.*

"Find them and get cured after accompanying me as I address the people upstairs."

Did she just somehow listen to my unspoken thoughts? "Yes, Your Grace."

After handing his stallion's reins to the blonde, Alysse and Randall then walked up the spiral stairwell in the back left corner to the third floor balcony, Alysse stepping out onto it while Randall remained inside.

The queen called for her people's attention, and windows creaked open.

"Law abiding citizens of Starkton, I, Queen Alysse Lilan-Sterling, announce that King Gwayne's Plague is ending thanks to your unwavering obedience. And as your reward, over the next few months every surviving adult in Starkton's tax records will receive three thousand gold coins, with an extra five hundred per child, to spend however you will."

Many cheers erupted from outside…while Alysse's upstairs workers slumped over inside.

"But at today's sunrise, Gwayne Sterling succumbed to his namesake plague. Yet during his final days, he kept high spirits and looked to Starkton's prosperity and peace we created, which will not continue under Drake's rule."

Why withhold this before now, and contest your son? The general wanted to ask as disagreement outside began and Alysse's workers smiled with open arms.

"I have served you every single day Starkton's been smothered, but has and will my son who hides in the White-Grey Keep? And will he honor your pay from your Crown? My son Drake Sterling may be the natural heir to Gwayne's throne, but I, Alysse Lilan-Sterling, am the better monarch and your rightful heir."

General Randall Bilteen gritted his teeth with closed lips as chaos erupted outside. *Alysse, I love and support you, but the High King will make you answer for this treason and starting another civil war, Your Grace.* He wanted to speak his mind, yet coughed without control instead.

Queen Alysse Lilan-Sterling turned to her winded general, walked slow to him and consoled "Abelot's already won me Lesirion Strigil's support." She then walked past, turned around and whispered "I love you too" with a serpentine smile before continuing her walk to the stairwell.

The once stoic general stared at his queen in horror.

REFLECTION

The Sword Maiden's soul danced once again to the Golden Dragon's drumbeat; however, he did not dance with her, but the snow smothering Dragon Fall did. *Why is Abelot heeding his swordsmanship over my intimations? At least he's staying prepared and not slacking in arrogance.* Samantha Starlight meditated upon her relationship with Abelot Wyvern, visualizing their sword training in Dragon Fall's thick untrailed snow.

How many must die to starvation, hypothermia, and opened throats before Farquad surrenders? Samantha looked beneath a blanket behind her cot at stashed rations and checked the leather lining of her steel armor before gazing to the woods. *Am I as guilty as he?* Samantha peered to the siege. *Not if I do right.* She then walked amongst her allied forces and found work until evening.

A King's Wisdom

Later that evening, Samantha snuck to Abelot's round tent bearing a basket holding two bottles of riesling, stainless steel goblets, one wheel of white provolone cheese and one of orange and white colby jack. As she silently opened the entrance flap, Samantha embraced smoke and warmth from a small sandalwood fire beneath a ventilation hole in the roof and relaxed her shoulders. Her sincere smile grew at Abelot wearing humble underclothing whilst sitting upon a fur blanket sharpening Morning Glory. *Never did I think I'd see Sir Abelot wearing something other than his signature armor, but I wish it was something more lordly.* Abelot kept working and ignored her. He needs to relax for once.

Ting! Ting! Ting! Samantha tapped a wine bottle with a goblet and caught Abelot's attention. "If I was an assassin, you'd be dead right now."

Abelot laid his sword upon the bed. "I-I-I w-w-was wo-wo-working on m-m-m...my sword I w-was hold-d-d-ding, so you-you-you'd have died too." He smiled. "Wh-wh-what brings you h-h-h-h...here th-this evening?"

Samantha raised her basket and cooed "Fierce warriors need to rest and refresh." while plopping down beside him. Her midnight eyes became star-spangled universes reflecting Abelot's fire as their sun, Abelot Wyvern their Sun God. "Would you rather have the provolone or colby jack?"

Abelot eyeballed the cheese wheels, grabbed the colby jack wheel and sliced it. "How did you know my favorite cheeses?" he asked in enthusiasm.

It looks like he's eating part of his chest armor, Samantha noticed as she ate provolone slices. "You told me during the evening you grilled those steaks marinated in brown-sugared bourbon..." Her smile grew. "...when you were deep in the cups with Valus and Apple-Eye, your stutter mostly gone."

Abelot tilted his head after swallowing some riesling. "What enticed this memory?"

Samantha leaned closer to him. "Your cooking is delicious, and everyone had a good time."

"Thank you." Abelot drank some more. "I privately recorded recipes from award-winning restaurants and bakeries."

Yes, the small details I remembered are working in my favor, and his stutter's alleviating! Her divine face blushed. "Are there any other skilled cooks in your family?"

"The women uphold that tradition."

If we were to marry, would he expect me to trade my armor for a dress? "Understood; now tell me something else about your family."

"House Wyvern? I thought you'd want to ask me about something interesting."

"There are lots of interesting things to learn from history. Start from the origin of your House, if you can."

"My mother told my siblings and I when we children that as some of our ancestors fled the Elven-Goblin skirmish over this territory, they witnessed Dubuver's body crash from the heavens, reducing to bones while fire burned all 'round." Abelot pointed to his cuirass. "My sigil is tied to your home's origin."

"It's a shame the Elves lost the Battle of Dragon Fall and went extinct while the Goblins continued reigning terror."

"Until my grandfather returned the karma! I don't remember much about 'who begat who,' but my grandfather Leggeron the Stern became a Latran Wolves mercenary, and during a goblin-hunting contract he travelled to Long Harvest, attended the annual Tournament of Grains and met my grandmother Olenna Skycloud, the tournament's ritual dancer."

Samantha perked up. "I met Olenna and her siblings Alexander, Micah, and Sharon as a young girl before they all left this world, but never met your great-grandfather Cardin Skycloud or anyone of Wyvern blood."

Abelot reciprocated Samantha's enthusiasm. "I barely knew my grandmother. What do you remember of her?"

"Not only was your grandmother kind to me, she baked delicious pastries that even the High King sought when he'd visit Long Harvest. *But Olenna isn't the only mentionable Skycloud.* Her brother Micah's children Brandon and Sandra gained more of Long Harvest's favor when they stopped some bandits from poisoning a village well." Samantha sighed and rolled her eyes. "And my betrothal to Brandon's son whose name I shall not say fell apart though I believed for a while that he was sent by the Battlemage." *I wish he had sincerely loved me instead of toyed with my emotions and slept with numerous other women behind my back.* She sighed again. "But what is meant to be is what is meant to be." Samantha held back tears while she and Abelot finished drinking.

"I-indeed you are correct."

With heart and stomach trying to escape their mobile prison, Samantha placed one hand on Abelot's knee. "What about you? I've never seen you embrace a woman nor heard talk of one."

There were dark pits in Abelot's eyes where light should have beamed. "W-women scorn m-m-m-my heart yet neither m-m-my body n-nor..."

Samantha shook his knee. "Quit lying to yourself. If your heart is scorned, then why did I hear your name praised in Starkton's streets? Sex may come cheap to those gifted with good looks, money, and intellect; but who in this world hasn't found those attributes attractive?" Samantha leaned in closer. "True love with the right God-given person is priceless when patiently discovered." Her nose twitched. "If you truly believe your heart is scorned, then why have I deemed you worthy of my affection, even after you broke my nose in the tavern?"

"P-p-p-p-please forgive my harm d-d-done."

It is finally working. Samantha wrapped her arms around Abelot's shoulders and appreciated the warmth and strength of his relaxing body as her curved chest pressed against his. "I already have, for your character is unparalleled, yet our lives seem parallel with few differences, as if we were destined to meet..." Her speech reduced to a whisper as she finished with "...as if we were destined to love each other." Thus the Sword Maiden kissed the Golden Dragon, savoring the exhilaration of her lover's tongue dancing within her mouth against hers as she helped him remove his shirt and the ornate necklace underneath.

OMEGA

*T*his darkness is welcoming, but where am I? Abelot stopped staring at the empty sky above and analyzed the autumnal forest around him. "Is anyone nearby?" *Wheeeshooooo!* Abelot's armor chilled from a sudden gust as orange, yellow, and red leaves danced to the ardent forest floor. "Why is everything as clear and colorful as a painting?" Another breeze danced, whispered, and further chilled his gilt armor as Abelot gazed upon the darkness again, shivering. *This is neither the hour of owls or stars.* His shiver worsened. "I need to build a fire before this weather cools further." Eyeing the trees around him and an adequate place for a fire pit, the knight reached for his sword, but found it missing. *I'll have to dig by hand and break off wood, but can I at least start a fire?* He then searched for tinder, rocks, and fallen branches…

...Until the ground began vibrating, and approaching footsteps accompanied indecipherable whispers.

As the quaking intensified from cloaked figures approaching from all directions, the Golden Dragon grabbed a fallen tree limb and braced himself. "Who are you?!" he called when they circled him as the air wintered. *Of all the times I need my sword, I am missing it during probably the worst.* Abelot studied them. Led by one carrying an ornamental battle axe, some carried flaming lanterns while others bore pointed ears poking out beneath their hood.

With a leathered voice, the one holding the battle axe said "Your birth cry declared the warrior you have become." The speaker pulled back his hood to reveal a face almost identical to Abelot's except bearing a grizzled beard, and sapphire eyes matching Abelot's.

"Who are you?"

"We are your ancestors."

You cannot fool me. "Did you win your battle axe from slaying a minotaur?"

"Does the goblin-spawn wear Brask Latran's blooded cape he pried off my body?"

For a silent minute, tears of rage froze on Abelot's face before he nodded, then knelt. "I am honored to meet you, Grandfather." *Is this the afterlife, or something else?*

Leggeron's face remained stoic. "Knighthood outshines my unfinished legacy."

"You believe it's unfinished through Valus? He may be gruff and deformed, but isn't a wretched goblin."

Leggeron pointed to his eyes.

"You're claiming Valus' eyes are yellow because he's descended from goblins? Have you no further evidence to this goblin heritage allegation?"

"House Vinearkh was the Latran Wolves' primary client for Grecan goblin hunts, where I met Valus and the Vinearkhs' castle warlock Pegasus, both of whom joined my goblin-hunting party. Valus' great-grandmother Mavra was captured and used by a goblin shaman named Seed, until she fled to Dragon Fall pregnant and my party slew him after he transformed into a dragon through magic. At Dragon Fall, Mavra discovered a way to weaken the goblin germination and begat Arthur the Militant bearing partial humanity. Arthur married a Grecan mountain lass and begat the further diluted Riesla and Arzat, whose incest then reversed the dilution through Valus. Dubuver created the Goblins to bring chaos into this world, and I regret my part in spreading it by sparing Valus for being a Wolf."

"No."

"What did you just say to me?!" Leggeron drew his axe. "WHAT DID YOU JUST SAY TO ME?!"

Abelot rose to his feet, approached Leggeron, and uttered "No. Ancestors and environment do not define the person, so if sparing my friend leaves your legacy unfinished, then so shall it be."

"You dare further dishonor us, Bastard?" asked another cloaked figure with a woman's voice. They and another unveiled themselves as a stone-eyed Winifred Catrain and Petyr Wyvern.

Abelot's irises transformed into cold flames. "Dishonor?! Had you not-."

"When I told you to work the docks, you started a smithy while selling your sword."

"I provide protection."

"How can you succeed in protection when your practices bring injury?"

"Controlling other people's choices is impossible, but if I weren't to suffer injuries during martial arts practice, I would have died in combat by now. Must I list my many successes in warfare, including *us* ending Cedric's streak of heinous crimes, against his own family nonetheless?"

"I told you to raise your own family, yet you still reside with your sister."

"My priorities are purposeful instead of conventional."

"Why does your resistance persist?"

I am my own person. "I choose to live. Did you?"

Petyr Wyvern condescended "You are no son of mine. You should've turned out like your brother."

"I warned my brother to prepare in the event of another attack, but his greed cost him his life."

"He served and died in the presence of the king. Your end will never amount to his."

"I was knighted by that same king."

"You knew before leaving town your brother wasn't a fighter like you. He's dead because you were not there to die in his place."

Abelot roared "AT LEAST I'M NOT DEAD YET!" and it echoed through the void. As the resonance became a whisper of "I'm dead," the void transitioned from black to white and Abelot's eyes reopened to his paramour cuddled against him. His penis hardened when her naked body rubbed against him while she awoke and stared into his eyes.

"You are great at keeping a lady's bed warm," Samantha purred. "Thank you, and good morning." She joined her lips to Abelot's and caressed his broad, chiseled shoulders as they engaged in passionate sex again before they prepared for battle and exited Abelot's tent.

As Abelot marched and Samantha bounced through Dragon Fall's thick snow, the multitude of tents and siege engines did not hasten the winds chilling their armor and soldiers covering frostbitten bodies. With dry hands stinging and spine and knee aching, he halted to rest against a scorpion's wheel, but Samantha dragged him into the leaders' pavilion indicated by Valus' destrier stabled beside.

Upon entry, Abelot's eyes burned from smoke staining the tapestried walls surrounding the crowded, Dragon Fall map-topped table where allies filled themselves with drink and meat. "You're an hour late. Explain before I put this knife in your eye." Apple-Eye scowled to the latecomers as he twirled his throwing knife, blood trickling onto his smoked steak. Samantha laughed while everyone stared in silence before all except Abelot, Valus and Apple-Eye joined her hoot.

Samantha grabbed Abelot's balling fist and retorted "We had to get warmed up lest we join the frozen we saw on our way here."

Valus' face soured further as he finished his drink and slammed his mug to the ground.

"If it makes you feel better…" The room fell silent as she leaned to the table, examined the map then tapped it. "Right here is an entrance to a tunnel where I played growing up."

Valus rose to his feet, spear in hand and barked "Your hesitation cost lives." He then turned to Apple-Eye and snarled "While I'm storming Dragon Fall with these two, you're going to defend our position and write to Lantheon's castellans announcing our victory, starting with my juvenile half-brother Thanksgiving."

"Yes, my lord, but once this usurpation concludes we best hide in the wilds until the High King's fury passes."

I am bold. Abelot frowned sharp. "I-I th-th-th…thought y-y-you w-w-w-were a wa-wa-warrior and n-n-n-not a c-c-c-coward. And-and K-K-K-King Gwayne or-or-ordered m-m-m-me to b-b-b-b…bring him r-r-reinforcements."

"Gwayne Sterling is dead."

I am reliable. "Drake w-will r-r-receive th-th-th-…the army in h-his st-st-st…stead."

Valus blurted "Marriage outweighs lineage."

I am honorable. "Y-y-you w-w-w-w-…would choose a h-h-harlot over an-an architect?"

Valus turned to Samantha, commanded her to lead the way, and gathered one hundred fifty savages who stank of regardless survival and purchasable loyalty.

After they traversed the blizzard and forestry, Samantha stopped at a foliaged mound cupped by hibernal wisterias and commanded its unmasking. Once Samantha's tunnel was unveiled, she and Valus descended into the fetid darkness first while Abelot entered last. "This is a mistake." Abelot whispered to roaring overhead waves while following silhouettes slipping on ice and clambering to webbed roots. *How old is this tunnel?* He stopped to light a torch, his eyes stinging with the revelation of caged, long-haired skeletons surrounded by smaller arrow-riddled skeletons tied to poles. *Did they embrace the afterlife, or fear it?* With no one else to answer Abelot's silent question, the tunnel's aquatic roars answered with increased volume.

And so did Abelot as he fell to his knees, tears filling his eyes as he pounded stones for an immeasurable period in solitude… until a child's voice said "Sammy needs you" and a small hand grabbed his.

Abelot swatted the hand away, turned and found human and Elven children bearing toys and one carrying Morning Glory. They ran, and surrendered the sword at a trapdoor where feminine screams screeched beyond. Abelot's stinging, blooded hand squeezed Morning Glory's hilt as he crept through and was greeted by dead soldiers laid against bone-hewn walls, wine barrels, and trailing further into Dragon Fall.

A King's Wisdom

Dragon Fall's corpse trail led into her great hall where an obese, tar-and-feathered nobleman lynched from upstairs watched the invaders ravish captured females and plunder the castle. *I thought my allies weren't fiends; is Samantha caught up in this?!* Abelot examined every horrifying detail of the room and found a surrounded, blood-lathered Valus Vinearkh beating on an upstairs door holding his spear in his inferior hand. Abelot approached the brutes then asked "Wh-where are Sa-Sa-Sa-Samantha and h-h-h-her mother?" while their failure to open the door repeated. Its eyehole opened and dark eyes peeked out.

"Where do you think?" Valus snarled as his semi-fingerless dominant hand pointed to the door.

"I th-th-th…thought you Wolves w-w-were ab-b-bove savagery."

Valus showed his maimed hand. "Samantha owes me, and we appreciate the spoils of conquest, as should you."

Abelot looked to Lord Farquad's corpse, the sacking, then back to Valus. "I am not a goblin."

Valus rapped the floor with his spear. "Before you join your grandfather in dying to my hand, would you like to watch us take turns with Samantha and her mother while she eats her amputated fingers?"

Abelot peeked to the midnight eyes staring from the door's eyehole, to Valus' entourage, and then stared into Valus' yellow eyes. "I don't think so."

The Golden Dragon then lunged forth, plucked out the Centaur's eye, and drew his sword against one hundred fifty-one Wolves.

SPIDERS

Grrrrr....

Brother Anton's stomach rumbled louder than his mare's metal shoes meeting stones on the forest floor. Countless days passed since he entered the divine labyrinth and left the designated path, finding scarce edible vegetation and fungi to prevent dipping into the saddlebags. It didn't take long for the horse's hay to deplete to dregs after reaching the Autumnal Ring. "How could I let this happen?" the monk asked the horse. He coughed dark yellow mucus. "Forgive me, dear friend." *This could have been over by now had we followed the road, and I need medicine.* He found a raspberry bush some birds were feeding on and picked a handful for the horse. It ate from his hand and neighed. He then picked some more and tossed them into the hay bag before continuing their impromptu trek.

Fallen branches and leaves crunched between the trees drying in perpetuity. "Why did I not wait until sunrise to continue following the road?" Brother Anton grumbled and coughed. "If we die he-"

CRACK! NEEEIIIIGGGGHHHH!!!! Brother Anton's mare lost its footing, tossing the monk as it fell. "The sword!" He checked his side and found Hadlia still sheathed. He gasped and coughed out more mucus. "And curse this foul plague!" he exclaimed, arising after climbing onto a fallen tree. The horse screeched its neighs. Brother Anton walked to the mare and investigated. Its broken leg bone protruded above the hole the horse stepped into.

The monk looked around. The road to Dragon Fall was nowhere nearby, and no smoke rose over the treetops. "Forgive me, my dear friend," Brother Anton wept as he unsheathed Hadlia and pierced the horse's heart. "May your eternal afterlife be pleasant," he saluted while horse blood soaked his clothing and the foliage. The monk moved the bags away from the pooling blood during the horse's final breaths and checked the inventory of the wearable satchel.

A dagger, dried meat and mushrooms, cannabis, a change of clothes, a rope, and a spell tome filled his bag. The monk grabbed the dagger and gathered tree limbs, leaves, and some rocks to build a fire and lean-to. Once the fire started, he then skinned the warm mare carcass and skewered cuts above the fire to cook and dry the meat, eating some portions as the rest shriveled and dried. After filling his bag with horse jerky, Brother Anton dragged away from his shelter what remained of the mare and rested for the evening.

A King's Wisdom

Dawn crept between the trees, and so did chest pain to the wakening monk. Brother Anton applied pressure to the scar covering his implanted amethyst stone as he grumbled, "Couldn't I have just pissed myself again?" But that anger transformed with his widening eyes as he struggled to blurt, "I'm not casting spells!" between congested coughs and scrambled to examine his makeshift shelter. Everything was intact. "This makes no sense! URGGH!" The pain brought him to his knees and shifted to a particular point. "Magic?!" He moved about, and so did the pain. "If something is leading me somewhere, then I shall follow."

The monk grabbed his equipment and followed the direction the chest pain directed, walking with ragged breaths and violent coughs for several miles over no trod path, landmark, or changing scenery until he reached trees with vined, rose-colored flowers hanging like moss. "Wisteria trees, in the Autumnal Ring?" Brother Anton rested for a few minutes and expelled more mucus before continuing to follow the magic signal until it led to two paths; one bearing rubbed trees with branches pruned and massive hoof prints in sets of two marking the soil beneath, the other being two separated rows of wisteria trees growing in ordered perfection.

The signal pointed to the ordered wisteria trees.

With a racing heart, Brother Anton stepped into the path and pressed forward. His heart eased as his body relaxed with the path's scent of patchouli and silence eliminated the chirps of distant birds. Not one animal dwelled along this path which led to an open floral grove circled by more wisteria trees. *Why am I here?* He looked around. A rusted iron helmet was beside a tree. The monk continued his search by following the edge of the grove…

Until it led to a charcoal-haired armored skeleton laid in a burial position with its head resting upon a rock and yew bow in its hands. Brother Anton prayed over the fallen archer and then further searched the body. As he gagged and sought forgiveness, the monk removed the skeleton's quiver, took its bow, and restored the body to a respectful position before praying again. His chest pain stopped. After searching the grove and finding nothing else of importance, he made his way back to the path.

Upon returning to the fork at midday, Brother Anton ate some of his reserves and studied the hoof prints. *How many deer have travelled this way?* He followed the hoof prints and watched for game. Rabbits and elk scurried over the foliage beneath mocking jays eating from blueberry bushes and the fruit trees lining the path. The monk stopped near a peach tree and grabbed one. As he was reaching for a second, the ambience changed, and he looked around. Several elk, deer, and birds stared. The monk turned his gaze back to the peach, retracted his hand, told himself "no," and continued down the path.

It opened to another grove, but this one was larger than the first and teemed with wildlife, bore a lake reflecting the magenta sunset, and wisteria trees made room for other tree species. *I could live here if I wasn't pursuing Abelot*, the monk presumed upon the sight of an ancient temple atop a hill overlooking the lake. *Am I the first person to discover this in millennia?* Only more dense forestry led to the temple. "UGH!" The monk grabbed his chest and kneeled as the magic pain returned with the pestilent coughs. "Whoever is speaking to me, I wish you would enlighten me more pleasantly!" he cried. Before he could get back up, Brother Anton stared at the ground. More hoof prints led to the forestry preceding his destination, so he followed within.

Many cut trees, armored and gowned skeletons of all shapes and sizes, and hoof prints littered the serene foliage beneath the temple's steep climb. The monk stopped and prayed over the handle of a buried weapon and bull's skull near a massive skeleton. Once Brother Anton finished his prayer, he called unto the skeletons, "May all your souls rest in peace" and continued his trek.

As Brother Anton finished tracking the hoof prints uphill, he was greeted by the temple crafted from moss-covered granite blocks chiseled into perfect cubes, and approached an archway beneath an awning supported by columns wrapped with spiraling aspen roots. Fading sunlight from a gape in the sanctuary's roof photosynthesized moss growing upon fallen beams and stones upon the natural floor. *I can repair this.* He stepped within. Pitch black doorways with cobwebbed candelabras lined the sides of the sanctuary. *I can relight and restore this place*, the monk concluded while lighting the candelabras with a wooden shard lit by *Fire…*

But who worshipped here? Two statues of Verítamor the Battlemage, one of stone holding a battle axe and the other of wood holding a bow, stood parallel upon the granite pulpit guarding its marble altar vined with dried roots and brass censers on both sides. "I heard Dwarves existed around the time of the 'Elven extinction' and rivaled them in many aspects, but I never imagined coexistence within sacred spaces." He turned to each doorway. Some had ascending stairs, others descending, others remaining ground level. "Respective living quarters for Elven and Dwarven acolytes?"

Brother Anton unsheathed Hadlia with his free hand before climbing an ascending stairway in caution. Moonlit windows and an open balcony lined the wall sharing the same building face as the pulpit downstairs, but the moonlight was subpar in lighting the abandoned barrack. Rotten bedframes adorned with cobwebs still upheld slumped straw mattresses. The monk investigated each bed. Brother Anton packed within his bag archaic tomes discovered under a few beds and prayed toward the moonlight. Upon opening his eyes following prayer, a firefly flew onto the balcony balustrade. He followed.

A handful of fireflies pulsed their light around the moonlit lake like twinkling stars surrounding a galaxy. *Where are the rest?* the tired, sick monk pondered unto the darkness of night. He had another coughing fit and leaned against the balustrade to expel more mucus before pissing off the balcony while looking around. The balcony wrapped around the building face, connecting to another room.

He stepped into the dark, his torch revealing a scribe's office with a bed in the corner and an unfinished book on a podium beside a shelf bearing jars of herbs. He flipped through the pages before removing one of the tomes from his sack. *I can finish this in due time*, he realized before adding it and a jar of cannabis to his growing collection and inspecting the bed. The bed was in better condition than the others in the barrack, so he lit the candelabras near the doorways and extinguished his torch before lying down for the night. As he placed his sword beside him, he prayed with eyes closed and slept...

Until loud breathing and hoof clops awoke him.

Brother Anton grabbed Hadlia and scanned the room for the threat. *Is it invisible?* he wondered when what caused the commotion did not reveal itself. He coughed "Show yourself." No response was given despite the breathing and movement continuing. *Something is either downstairs or outside.* The sick monk's esophagus itched just as another coughing fit began and he rushed to the balcony and spit dark yellow mucus to the ground below. *It picked up my scent*, he realized while searching for the threat, only to find the fireflies missing and clouds hiding the moon. The monk's cough persisted. *I'm in no condition to fight whatever is here*, Brother Anton concluded as he sheathed the sword and drew the bow. *I must somehow escape.*

Putting his back to the balustrade, Brother Anton peered to the barrack. The candelabras remained lit and no sign of what hunted him was present. *My scent is not as strong in this room as in the office.* He crept into the barrack, descended its staircase in silence and peered into the lit sanctuary.

Hoof! HRUGH! A nine-foot tall bullish humanoid with flowered horns on its head clopped its hooves throughout the sanctuary wielding a glowing gemstone hammer-axe onehanded. *A minotaur, like the ones mentioned in the Veridom's bestiary claiming hybrid*

Elven-Dwarven magic as the creature's origin; this must be what left the hoof prints I've been following and the bull skull and massive skeleton among the others, but they normally protect their tethered territory and unicorns. More clops came from the adjacent corner.

Remaining in the shadow of the doorway, Brother Anton peeked when the minotaur had its back turned. A snow white unicorn with a spiraled horn glowing atop its head lingered in the sanctuary corner. The monk ducked back in. *Why did I leave the room lit? My escape is becoming increasingly difficult! And I can't stay in one spot too long.* He crept back upstairs to the barrack and extinguished the flames lighting the room, watching the smoke rise within the dark. *I need a strategy or I'm dead.* The monk started having another coughing fit, driving him back to the balcony to expel more mucus over the balustrade.

Salvation is around you, a voice within Brother Anton's mind whispered.

"Show yourself," the monk commanded with bow knocked and back against the balustrade. No one was around. Smoke still billowed from the extinguished candelabras and light brightened the scribe's office, shining against the herbal jars. He coughed some more, eyes brightening as the minotaur's hoof clops echoed near the barrack stairway. *In my weakened state, I doubt one of my arrows could kill the beast, but perhaps I could stun it.* The monk slipped into the scribe's office stairway and reached into his bag.

Upon returning to the sanctuary, the minotaur remained focused on the barrack stairway as Brothern Anton crept to a censer and cast *Fire* upon the cannabis in his hand before dumping it into the censer and sneaking back to the stairway. As smoke began to billow from the censer, the monk tossed the jar at it, shattering the jar. The minotaur rushed to the censer and kneeled to it and the glass shards. *Now's my chance!* The pirate-turned-monk started for the door…

And so did the mucus for his respiratory. Adrenaline activated as Brother Anton peered to the altar. The minotaur got the censer's chains caught on its horn as it raised its head, stared at the fleeing man, and tightened its grip on the hammer-axe with its sprint. Brother Anton tossed aside his bow, quiver, and bag to increase his speed before reaching the sanctuary entrance and ducking aside as the minotaur sped past and chopped down a tree with one axe swing.

The pirate-turned-monk examined himself after his near-death experience. The only items he possessed to defend himself were the sword he scavenged in Fropilé and monk's habit he was wearing. *If I die tonight, then at least I will have in my hand a sword gained with divine intervention*, he acknowledged. Wind gusts waved his whitened hair and beard. *But I refuse to die to any beast other than a kraken of the sea,* Múto decided. He searched the forgotten battlefield of this magic grove, coughing as the minotaur began turning to him. A massive pile of tree limbs laid upon the fiery orange and red autumnal foliage on the opposite side of the hill. He ran to the brush pile and crawled within.

The pirate-turned-monk crawled past frightened snakes until he became trapped between tree limbs wrapping him in nocturnal darkness, struggling to breathe, thick coughs drawing closer the footsteps of the behemoth hunting him. The scent of burning cannabis lingered with stomach growls. *I am going to die alone, in the dark,* Brother Anton concluded as he writhed to the brush pile's edge and saw the grove's still lake. *At least my final sight is beautiful.*

"Never be afraid to ask for help," a familiar voice whispered.

"Koli, is that you? Where are you?" The pirate-turned-monk pushed against the gnarled branches and yelled "HHEEeeeellllllp!" His first yell was soft, the branches fell back, and his chest ached. "You mock me one last time?"

"Potentia," the voice whispered.

"Potentia?!" The pirate-turned-monk's chest pain intensified as more adrenaline coursed his veins and further accelerated blood flow with his slipping humanity. "RRREEEEWWWRRRRPPPP!" The next yell became an echoing snarl as he created an opening for escape. "RRRRREEEEWWRRRR!!!" The next yell was feral and rippled across the lake as wildlife froze in fear and the earth shook. Every yell grew louder and wilder as the pirate-turned-monk emerged from the natural tomb to challenge his magic foe.

Emitting earthshaking growls, saliva flooded Brother Anton's whitened beard while his lacrimal glands watered his cheeks during his advancement in shivering feral rage against the dazed minotaur now frozen in fear. The pirate-turned-monk's fingers curled into a fist just before the minotaur fled to the lake when he was four feet away from the beast. "That's what I thought," he taunted before returning to the sanctuary.

A King's Wisdom

Upon Brother Anton's return, his yew bow laid unbroken where he dropped it, yet the unicorn sniffed his bag. The monk reached within, fed the unicorn dried mushrooms, and petted it before mounting his new steed.

They left the sanctuary by way of the mass grave. "Do you know the way to Dragon Fall, by any chance?" Brother Anton asked the unicorn. As they exited the forest path between the sanctuary and grove, the moon was uncovered and fireflies returned and multiplied to light the grove to dawn visibility. "At least I can see now, but this doesn't lead me back to the road to Dragon Fall," Brother Anton exclaimed just before many fireflies straightened themselves into rows on the grass.

OUT OF BOND

I wish this storm would end," Stella Starlight repeated since dawn while sipping spiced wine, staring to the hibernal forestry across the lake, curling her nose to rising war ashes, listening to rasped breathing and her daughter vomiting. *Death surrounds me, and High King Lesirion will surely bring more, but those women I sent to the nearest convent won't be raped this time.* Coughs erupted, and Stella turned to the source.

Riddled with infected wounds, the slumbering Abelot Wyvern coughed blood upon his straw deathbed. Stella approached him and strong-gripped his hand. "I am grateful for you, and wish you'd wake up." Stella glanced to his immaculate sword laid upon the folded crimson cape on the bedside table. Tears welled within her eyes. "Keep fighting. Keep fi-."

Dun! Dun! Dun! Loud knocks rattled the door… followed by silence.

It's been at least seven days since my permitted knocked before entry, so that must be a straggler who hid, Lady Stella realized before she removed the garrote concealed within her bosom, slipped off her shoes and crept barefoot to the backside of the door. She cuffed her hands around her mouth and faced the window. "Who is it?"

A strained, familiar feminine voice responded "It's me, mother."

Stella relaxed, opened the door and left it open. "Gain any intelligence on their whereabouts?"

"There's still no trace of the Latran Wolves."

"Thomas Apple-Eye must have kept his word and fled to avoid Lesirion's army."

Samantha spat on the floor. "Or he's planning to attack after refreshing and restoring his band. He knows the location of the secret entryway into the wine cellar."

Another secret passage, and an outsider knew about it before me? "I'll have it guarded, but I don't think Apple-Eye is vicious like Valus turned out to be."

Loud, rushing metallic footsteps approached from down the hall, and then a soldier entered. "Pardon the intrusion, my ladies," they wheezed, "but a lone monk has arrived riding a unicorn."

Samantha blurted "Now is not the time for games. Return to your station."

"This is not a joke, Lady Samantha. He's stabling it."

After promising execution for perjury, the Sword Maiden brisk-walked away before returning with a sheathed bastard sword with golden quillons and a white-haired monk wearing a farmer's straw hat whose presence felt holy yet tainted. "The unicorn is real, and here is its master!" Samantha announced.

The stranger uncovered his head and bowed.

"It's a pleasure to meet you, milady, and thank you for the hospitality." he greeted. "I am Brother Anton, hailing from the Verídom of Fropilé in Tavuk to evangelize and heal." He glanced at the dying knight. "I reached Abelot just in time!" Just as the stranger began walking to Abelot, the soldier pressed a hand against his shoulder.

"Stop right there." the soldier commanded. "No one is to be in the presence of Dragon Fall's Hero without Lady Stella's permission."

"Abelot Wyvern and the Lantheon Realm need me." Brother Anton controlled his breathing and whispered "When I was training for mission work, I received divine visions showing two possible fates following today's circumstances. One was Abelot dying and a green dragon overtaking this land by sorcery."

"Then save him!" the ladies cried.

"But first, what was the other?" the soldier asked.

"The other was a golden dragon with a corrupted mind conquering this land by military."

Samantha rebuked "Abby would never turn evil after saving us."

Brother Anton then exposed his scarred chest. The ladies gasped. "That man tortured and tossed me into the ocean to die when he could have ended my life mercifully. Young lady, if you think it's impossible for one's bestial nature to overtake their humanity and vice versa, guess again."

Samantha's nose twitched.

"But I do forgive Abelot Wyvern and have an idea for a third fate."

Stella looked to Abelot, then back to the stranger. *Samantha may be right.* "Do you expect us to believe a pirate?"

"The pirate I was died against Abelot, and the monk I am is willing to die for Abelot. I know a ritual which could give him my life, the life I don't deserve."

There must be another way to save Abelot, Lady Stella contemplated before piping "Life is precious. Why sacrifice it for a murderous opponent?"

The monk peered into Stella's eyes and stated "Freedom." He then examined Abelot's ruination and the window. "Time is of the essence. Let us pray before *he* gets here…"

Samantha asked "Who is coming?"

Rumbling ensued beyond the window, and all except the monk rushed to it. Across the lake, the Three Seasons Forest disappeared behind an encroaching army thousands strong bearing House Bilteen's topaz fox banners. And where Dragon Fall's drawbridge could lower approached an old, lone fox on his silver stallion. He then descended onto the snow in grace, enshrouded in silence while he stood militant as Stella, Samantha, and the soldier stared through the window.

The soldier placed their hand upon Samantha's shoulder, and then she swiped it away. "Stay with your mother, Lady Samantha. No one wants to see you and your unborn slain if General Bilteen storms Dragon Fall once the bridge is lowered."

Please don't think of fighting, Lady Stella wanted to say yet spoke "Randall Bilteen is renowned for his upstanding character and keeping oath. He deserves an honorable death."

"You may use my sword." the monk responded; the Sword Maiden nodded in return, and as she left for Dragon Fall's drawbridge, the soldier followed. While they met the general, muffled sounds of suffocation came from behind.

"General Bilteen." Samantha acknowledged in clarity.

Randall scanned the snow-covered skeletal fortress, and then responded in equal clarity "It has been brought to High King Lesirion Strigil's attention that House Starlight has captured Dragon Fall, which rightfully belongs to House Strigil, and Starkton's Golden Dragon and the Latran Wolves mercenary company participated in that affair. Surrender in peace his castle and my knight and none will be executed for treason today."

Samantha held her hand over her womb. "Sir Abelot Wyvern fulfilled his duty to your king by gaining House Starlight's alliance when he helped us reclaim our home." She unsheathed Brother Anton's bastard sword for all to bear witness its dark crimson blade with a deep cobalt fuller and ultramarine V-shaped stripes. "House

Starlight demands a trial by combat." Samantha tapped her womb. "*We* are House Starlight's champion."

Randall Bilteen stared upon her stomach with disappointment, spoke inaudible words, drew his sword and advanced...

Until he dropped it while grabbing for his heart as he fell onto the snow before lying motionless. Samantha checked him in caution, only for neither flinch nor sound to come from the old knight...

But a loud breath came from behind Lady Stella who immediately turned around. Abelot Wyvern's eyes were open, wounds cleansed and scabbed, flexing his hands while checking his body as Stella sprinted tear-eyed to him and hugged him breathless.

"Welcome back." the pirate-turned-monk greeted with clapping hands. Then confusion overtook him as he met Stella's gaze. "My lady, whose soul fulfilled the Resurrection Ritual?"

Stella responded with "There's something you two need to see." then helped Abelot to the window with the monk's assistance.

Tears streamed down Abelot's face, and he whispered "I wish this storm would end."

MERCY

The gods wept that day.

It was mid-evening when Sir Abelot Wyvern emerged from the Three Seasons Forest unaccompanied one mile ahead of Drake's reinforcements earlier intended for King Gwayne, damp from encumbrance and a storm stretching to Titan Bay. As he arrived to a northwestern countryside hill, Abelot clambered off his unicorn before dragging it to the brow overlooking Starkton's township.

Abelot's crooked nose curled, for his helmet could not filter the thick smoke further darkening the sky and blanketing Starkton's corpse piles. *Have I returned home, or did I ride straight into Hell?* Further north towards the roads to Honet and the White-Grey Keep sat an army bearing House Strigil's white owl on blue, House Lilan's white rabbit on scarlet, and House Bilteen's burgundy fox upon the banners outside their tents. *Oh, how I hate to see friends turn foe!* "Th-this is a shame." Abelot scanned Titan Bay. Robert Bilteen's fleet landlocked Starkton and surrounded *Silver Hare*. *No naval warfare, no maritime trade, better control of the plague; peacekeeping just like his father would. What about Rickard? And who will Drake's "Silver Foxes" serve once this war is over?*

Rustling noises crept from the direction of Alysse's Brothel. Abelot turned his gaze toward the brothel-turned-castle surrounded by a dying civilization. Unrecognizable charred bodies greeted him with decaying smiles. Abelot's heart raced as his penis hardened when visions of the brothel's vicious pleasures and perpetual intemperance flooded his mind. *Something evil coalesces here now, something my king cannot overcome alone.*

"No." Abelot responded in unison with his unicorn's whinny.

Abelot's heartbeat increased as he clenched his sword hilt in lightening rain. "I am the white dragon Verítamor sent to incinerate the treachery befallen unto Starkton. Has my honorable tree bore rotten fruit?" Abelot unsheathed Morning Glory, its blade reflecting the flaming facade his armor. "Whoever, or whatever, you are, I reject your offer and will see you struck down, even if I must give my life to watch you die!"

"Good luck with that" came from a crude male voice climbing the hill. "But then again I think that's the first anyone in town's heard you stutter-free. Did you take talkin' lessons while you were gone?" A potbellied commoner wearing a chainmail coif and House Lilan waffenrock climbed to meet the tip of Abelot's bastard sword wielding spade and Strigil banner. "Starkton's gone all to hell since ye went off again. And where did you get a unicorn?! I thought you went mad and tied a horn to your horse!"

Abelot lowered his sword. "Y-y-y-you're b-b-b-b-better off throwing Maidron's tankards th-th…than slinging that shovel, Jon. You call that a weapon?"

"I sharpen its edges and tip between skirmishes. It's all I got left after this war started besides the pitchfork Jorge is using."

"Your farm?"

Jon turned his head to the army for a split second. "You know how much *they* eat?" He eyed Abelot's cuirass. "You of all people ought to understand supplying limitless needs."

Abelot knocked his cuirass. "Indeed I do."

"It's a shame we're meeting here wielding weapons instead of mugs. Maidron's making bank from both sides right now, the Prancing Fox being 'off limits' from the daily fights."

"Anywhere else?"

"Nobody has dared desecrate the chapel where you were knighted, but I think it's because of the monks curing sick and healing wounded there; and Queen Alysse welcomes empty-handed brothel visits. No offense, but I heard your sister is sheltering there."

Abelot gave a dainty turn of his head to the hoof beats from the forest. "None taken." Abelot's brow furrowed. "How'd you kn-know I w-w-w-was coming t-t-t…to this hill?"

"I was sent to parley with the prince and was told this was a good spot for a highborn to sneak and plan for attack, so I came and you just happened to be here." Jon reached under his tunic and removed a wet letter. "I also need someone to read him this letter written by the high king."

Abelot looked to Drake's army stationed outside the White and Grey Keep's drawbridge. "You're going the wrong direction."

"I'm only following orders."

"Following orders?! You're running."

Jon murmured "fine, you got me. One of the high king's lieutenants thought that if anyone should die if the parley sours, it should be a local lowborn farmer to make Prince Drake look bad."

"Caught deserters face execution."

Abelot raised his sword.

"Don't kill me!"

With one swing of his sword, Abelot chopped in half Jon's banner pole, the banner falling onto mud. "Not today. Give me that letter, your colors, and head to Long Harvest." Jon obeyed and sprinted southwest as Abelot sheathed Morning Glory, threw the waffenrock at the banner and petted his unicorn. The march of his reinforcements grew louder.

How many more neighbors can I save? How long will it take to rebuild and improve Starkton? Abelot gazed into the eyes of his unicorn. "Does our opposition think King Drake is naïve?" *High King Lesirion Strigil doubtless wants my head after my involvement in the siege.* Abelot crinkled the parley letter with one hand. *Lies and half-truths intended to invoke complacency.* Two cavalrymen, one of House Starlight, the other a

Silver Fox, rode up the hill. *But I will not destroy this letter if my king, a better man and leader, wishes to read it.*

"Sir Abelot," the Starlight cavalryman called as he saw the Strigil banner and Lilan waffenrock on the mud before his horse defecated on them, "our enemies may have great numbers but we have greater warriors."

The Silver Fox eyed Abelot's letter. "Should we group with Drake's men or camp here?"

Abelot thumbed the crinkled letter. "Him." The three waited until the rest of Abelot's band arrived before marching in unison to Drake's forces, where they set camp outside the White and Grey Keep and sent Drake the confiscated letter. Drake's continued defiance to Lesirion and Alysse's demands created for his army the opportunity to settle down one more time before the next battle.

Excluding campfires warming and drying the brothers of war, midnight concealed warfare's travesties faster than the castle's periwinkle waters flowed through its waterwheels. Peripheral heat from the fire outside Abelot's tent felt ever more pleasurable as he loosened his armor and sipped from a cask of diluted wine. With sword nearby, steed tied outside his tent, and having already relieved himself for the night, Abelot lied down and closed his eyes.

Though he tried resting, Abelot's mind remained alert as he changed positions and restless soldiers chattered nearby. *Tomorrow's morning sun shall shine glorious, for righteousness is victor and not victim; though some of my neighbors shall leave this world, they will do so in an honorable manner.* Abelot positioned his pillow so it supported his neck.

A King's Wisdom

CRAACCKK! A loud crunch and discreet footsteps slipped from a nearby tent. Abelot pulled back his shoulder blades to release thoracic tension as he further relaxed his shoulders.

Spilling liquid noises came from the direction of the campfire outside Abelot's tent. *I'm thankful I avoided a hangover, unless that was someone putting out the fire.*

NNNNEEEEIIIGGGGHHHH!!!!! NNNNEEEEEEIIIIIGGGGHHHHH!!!!!! Every equine throughout the camp panicked as shouts erupted, swords sang war tunes and an adrenal Abelot scrambled to re-armor and grab Morning Glory. As Abelot exited his tent, soldiers with slit throats lied in a blood puddle extinguishing the campfire amidst blazing tents and his tethered unicorn kicked and screeched. Abelot slashed the reigns, and they joined the nocturnal battle.

Four Lilan infantrymen and a Strigil captain ganged around a wounded Sterling spearman fighting over the fallen. Abelot pointed his sword to the captain's heart and extended, countered their parry and pierced their right lung. Abelot stepped back, focused on the next soldier rushing him, and stepped aside before amputating their leg and impaling them as they panicked and flailed in their own blood. *What fodder!* Abelot smiled at two of them struggling against the spearman and the third fleeing as Abelot distracted one for his ally to eliminate before killing the other. Together, they gave the final soldier of that small group a swift end.

"Alysse's soldiers lack skill," Abelot smirked.

The soldier did not return cockiness. "Warfare was not their trade." He sprinted deeper into the conflict without hesitation.

Still vibrating from adrenaline, Abelot glanced upon his latest victims. *The baker across my smithy, the cobbler down the street, and two tavern workers; what have I done?* He found a box and climbed atop. Beyond the tents, fallen soldiers lied everywhere amidst those still fighting. *This surprise attack must have given Alysse the leverage she needs to defeat Drake, and Lesirion already knows about my involvement with his cousins' death.* Abelot gritted his teeth and held Morning Glory high. "I-if they want my home and head, th-they'll have to co-"

NEEEIIGH!

Abelot rushed to the nearby horse's aid. His unicorn, missing its spiraled horn and covered with deep gashes oozing silver-blue blood, was drowning in its blood puddle. *Who would dare harm such an innocent being?* Abelot looked around. A dead Strigil soldier, covered in bruises with the horn impaled in their neck, lied near other fallen soldiers from both sides, some whose brain matter was exposed through massive breaks in their skull. Abelot gazed upon the dying beast again, knelt in its blood, petted it and wept.

"You did not deserve this fate, m-m-m-my dear friend" Abelot consoled before towering his steed and placing Morning Glory's tip over its heart. "M-m-m-m...may you r-r-r-r-rest in peace and em-m-m-mbrace a p-p-p-p...pleasant afterlife," Abelot blessed before impaling the unicorn's heart. The unicorn's eyes rolled back as its breathing ceased...

A King's Wisdom

...Along with the sounds of war. Abelot's skin chilled, goosebumps riddling his arms. He looked around. Fighting soldiers froze in place amidst crystallizing flames and suspended arrows. Abelot turned back to the dead unicorn, his heart ready to explode as he gazed past.

An unblemished elf, reflecting galaxies within its eyes, stood past Abelot's unicorn wielding an aspen staff bearing a carved diamond, their robe matching the unicorn's blood and hemmed with crimson. With a double-frequent feminine and masculine voice, it boomed, "Thou hast honed thine blade with mine holy implement, o descendant mine." The staff's diamond glowed. "I declare all whom witness these words allow limitations to become limitlessness, foolishness into wisdom, cowardice into confidence, scarcity into abundance, past errs never hinder future successes." Abelot's sword glowed gold as fire swirled upward from the unicorn's heart. "May this godless land be cleansed by dragon fire!"

The elf disappeared, time unfroze, the unicorn's flame extinguished and Morning Glory dimmed and transformed from a bastard blade resembling its namesake flower into a thick great sword matching Abelot's armor. He grabbed its hilt dual-handed, his biceps and triceps tensing against the added weight. *This blade is no longer Morning Glory and needs a new identity.* Abelot hesitated until he remembered who he was. "Dragon Fire." A large open battle ensued beyond the flaming tents. Sprinting to it, Abelot called out "MAY GODLESSNESS BE CLEANSED BY DRAGON FIRE!"

Abelot's adrenaline never ceased whereas his breathing steadied in tune with the trickle of time. Facing an enemy mob, Abelot swung Dragon Fire against them, felling at least twenty-five with that first swing of his new celestial tool, their blood raining as he spun while tossing another soldier to his allies. *I didn't feel the impact resistance*, Abelot realized as he refaced the proper direction and cut a Strigil soldier in half. *May their suffering be short.* The opposition still had over four times as many soldiers, but Abelot continued hacking and slashing alongside his allies.

Before long, Drake's dwindling army continued their underdog push against Alysse's forces as dawn's peach luminescence crept over the battlefield. Abelot, already having defeated over eight hundred opponents, struggled to march forth and swing his great sword. Whoever dared climb a body pile hiding the chrysanthemums left themselves open to meeting their end, but Abelot never dared follow that beaten path, instead flanking those macabre barricades to even the odds.

Can we finish this? Abelot wondered before looking to the tree line. Beyond several hundred soldiers perched eight knights in elaborate Strigil armor surrounding a like-armored man on a white mustang and a general in Bilteen armor. *Lesirion Strigil and Rickard Bilteen.* Abelot gritted his teeth. *If we take Lesirion out, we cut off the head of this snake, but I will spare Rickard if possible.*

"Abelot!" He turned. Drake's army parted to let him through. "There that tall talk is. After everything he and my mother have done to my kingdom, I'm taking his crown." King Drake pointed his sword to the sky and screamed "IT'S NOW OR NEVER!" as his sword reflected the sunshine. The army emitted a feral roar, and with it…

…the second wind of Alysse and Lesirion's army. Rickard's cavalry slammed Drake's army with spears as Abelot braced himself and guarded King Drake. Drake commanded his units to brace themselves for further impact as his shield-bearers advanced to the frontline and opportunists unhorsed cavalrymen. To their dismay, some intelligent cavalrymen combined efforts to overwhelm individual shield-bearers to once again create an opening. King Drake heartily squeezed Abelot's shoulder as he saluted, "It's been a pleasure to fight alongside you, my revered knight."

Abelot stared to the waving shrubbery edging the tree line past the opposing generals. "Do you feel wind?" he asked.

"I don't." Drake returned.

Archers emerged, led by one wearing a crimson eyepatch. Abelot grabbed a shield from one of the slain shield-bearers and barricaded the king, graving, "It's b-b-b-b-been a pl-pl-pleasure fighting alllll…longside you, my king" just before the archer's rain fell.

FAITHLESS PURSUITS

Coital noises echoed throughout the lobby of Alysse's Brothel as Sable's instrumental rendition of "Nocturnal Lovers' Serenade" on a pine lyre with a wooden pick failed to smother the racket. *Six men, one of them being Mace.* Sable shook her head to the rhythm of the song. *Her godless actions are an insult to the sick and dying outside these walls.* Sable's music continued without error. *But then again this queen is also a prostitute by trade. Was she seeing Mace behind Gwayne's back before he died?*

Not one person in the lobby showed symptoms of the plague, nor were any injured present. Sable eyed a door kept under constant surveil, its door locked. *Why was I not given free access to the repurposed storeroom despite my partial ownership of this business?* Sable's fingers shook, causing her to get a cut on her left ring finger. *Are Alysse and Mace hiding someth-*

The door opened. Three Bilteen soldiers and one Strigil officer padded to their stations in tune with the finale of "Nocturnal Lovers' Serenade." *Playing another song does not feel right. I am tired of distracting this lot from where attention should be focused; who is paying the price for our tainted utopia?*

Sable's skin crawled.

Everyone in the lobby froze, eyes piercing through Sable as coital noises reverberated from other rooms of the brothel-turned-castle. The soldiers who bedded Alysse retained no evidence of humanity as they stared into unknown distances in silence. *Something wicked must be dwelling within this unholy place!* A drop of blood from Sable's finger landed upon the stone floor's mint rushes, crimsoning only the rushes but not the stone. "Play us another," a feminine voice called from the room. Queen Alysse, already cleaned and clothed, stood beneath the doorframe blushed-face while a fetching, olive-skinned man crowned with sun-dyed waves braided her auburn hair.

Does she not see my finger and know I need rest? "Your Grace, I have played so many songs that I don't know what to play next."

"Daisies and Cotton," Mace Doran suggested from within the shadow of Alysse's office. "Do you know it?"

"I do not." *You snake.*

"It's an upbeat tune popular amongst Honet's brothels and taverns," charmed the young man as he entered the lobby with the top two buttons of his doublet unbuttoned. The fine linens of nobility he wore complimented his bergamot perfume and smoked caramel eyes. "Honetian ladies love when I play it." He stepped toward Sable and leaned forward. A golden chain adorned with a pick dangled. "Must the legendary Rhaelyn the Honeyed teach with his famous lyre the tantalizing 'Daisies and Cotton' to an esteemed harpist?" Rhaelyn's eyes sparkled when he placed his hands upon Sable's still holding the instrument. "I won't ask for much in return."

Esteemed amongst dens of iniquity. Sable pulled back her hands as she returned the lyre. "Play it for us."

"Indeed I will." Thus Rhaelyn the Honeyed placed his fingers between and upon particular frets of his lyre's neck and strummed its strings using his fingers instead of a wooden pick, catalyzing warmer vibrations than a pick ever could. As the musician continued his hypnotic serenade, Mace Doran whispered in his ear and slipped him a golden jeweled necklace before taking seat near the office.

A silk hand slid across Sable's shoulder. "Such a talented fellow," Crystabella purred as she sat next to Sable. "But not masculine like Abelot. I need someone like your brother in my life…" Crystabella then sat upon Sable's lap, facing her. "…or better yet, you."

Sable's heart raced.

"I am wise in your wildest fantasies." Crystabella slid her hand onto Sable's inner thigh. "Allow me to ease your pressured mind."

Sable's face reddened. "Uummm…" Crystabella leaned in and locked her lips with Sable's. As Crystabella had her tongue gyrating against Sable's, Sable returned the action. *This feels fun, but not right,* she contemplated as they continued with the rhythm of Rhaelyn the Honeyed's rendition of "Daisies and Cotton" picking up pace. When Crystabella put her hands around Sable's waist, Sable returned it.

Crystabella stared into Sable's eyes and gestured to the room beside Queen Alysse's office. "Over here," she commanded as she led Sable within the moon-and-candlelit room. Crystabella closed the door. "Is this your first time with another woman?" asking as they undressed each other.

"Y-yes ma'am." *What am I doing, partaking in depravity?*

"Interesting." Crystabella lied with Sable on the bed in the corner of the room and began pleasing her.

This is fun. Sable embraced Crystabella's actions as she placed her head against the adjacent wall, a soft spot compared to the hard edges surrounding it. *Someone must have knocked a hole between these studs, and it wasn't properly repaired unless it's like this on purpose.* What sounded like walking and a door closing came from the other side. *Did the queen just enter that room?* Sable glanced at Crystabella, who paid no mind to said noises.

"Tell me you're joking," a feminine voice inquired.

The queen?

"No, for I depart," a masculine voice returned. "The boy knows nothing of my 'gift,' for his ignorant sacrifice is my known safety."

Mace, talking with the queen? It must be since the adjacent room is her office, and the voices sound like theirs.

"One like I gave to control Abelot?"

No, I do not believe this.

"Yes, Your Grace."

"But mine somehow failed me."

"If you look beyond these walls, you will see mine won't. We will reunite later, but for now, goodbye my love."

"Goodbye." Footsteps led to the direction of that office's door which opened and closed.

What more evidence can I uncover? Sable looked back between her thighs at Crystabella. *I need to continue my ruse if I wish to proceed investigation.*

"What's on your mind?" came from the voice below.

Sable turned to the moonlit window. "My brother."

"Knowing that warrior, he's resting before the next battle. We're lucky we don't have to fight."

"We are weaponless within these walls, restricted from communication and barred access beyond." Candlewax melted to each lit candle's base, their wax reflecting the women, some mirroring Sable's grey irises. "How is our present condition considered 'lucky?'"

Crystabella sat silent.

"We are being made complacent and weak within comf-"

The door flew open. "I beg your pardon?" inquired Queen Alysse from the doorway.

Crystabella turned to the whore-queen, back to Sable, again to Alysse. "She jests."

"Keep it that way." Alysse returned to the lobby.

"Forgive me, honey," Crystabella slunk away from the bed, "but I think it's time for us to end this tryst."

"Yes," Sable agreed as she joined in preparing to rejoin the others in the lobby. *At least I don't have to step out of my comfort zone any further than I did.*

Sable froze when the brothel's new stench defiled her nostrils.

Rhaelyn's entertainment continued amidst the crowd in the lobby, but now every one of the incumbents indulged in sweets, moonshine, and hallucinogens. *Was all this hidden within the provisions?* Sable pondered as consumption reached intemperance and sinners reveled, excluding those whose inebriation caused lethargy. Sable frowned at the guarded door concealing the provisions. *They choose godlessness over godliness, living purposeless instead of purposefully. I regret my contributions to this foolish self-deprecation.*

A silk hand clutched Sable's shoulder once again. *Really, Crystabella?*

Sable turned and met Queen Alysse's gaze. "Come with me." The queen escorted Sable into the candlelit office and closed the door behind them. "Explain your abstinence."

Explain my discipline. Sable held her cut ring finger near a candle, its warmth caressing the wound. "I beg your pardon, Your Grace?"

Queen Alysse gnashed her teeth and eyed the door. "You refrain from the festivities and slander my work."

I am maintaining a clear mind as best I can amidst distractions.
"Don't you recall Crys-"

"She did all I asked."

Sable's eyes widened. "So have I."

"You lie, songstress."

"By not playing a song I know not?"

"By your refusal to conform."

By refusing to blindly submit to hedonistic deception and self-destruction.
Sable studied the candles spread around. "Where did the sweets, moonshine, and hallucinogens come from?"

"I am the queen. Questioning me is not your place."

"It seems you have forgotten I partially own this retreat of carnal fantasies." *A sin I regret.*

"Listen to the words you just said, '*retreat of carnal fantasies.*' Would the extra commodities not fit within that definition?"

"Weakening everyone in this building during a war *you* started is not going to make this any better."

"And you have a better idea, or another to regret?"

Regret? Can Starkton's queen somehow read my thoughts, or just my mental reflections and things I refrain from speaking aloud? Sable paused against her racing heart, staring at the queen and analyzing the room in periphery as her shadow flickered on the beech boards covering the window. *Or am I overthinking?* With controlled breathing, Sable slung a couple candles onto the mint rushes covering the brothel floor and uttered "a better idea" as flames engulfed Alysse's office. *Even if I lose my life for the right cause.*

"How dare you!" screamed the queen as she struggled to pry the boards off the window, flames scorching and tearing her dress asunder. "I sheltered you, and this is how you treat me?!" she screamed at Sable unlocking the door.

"How dare I choose righteousness over iniquity! How dare I choose truth over lies! How dare I choose health over illness! How dare you be a witch in disguise!" Sable escaped into the lobby as the flames consumed the ground floor and surrounded the dragon statue. Many sprinted for the front door and bottlenecked themselves, burning alive while the entrance caved in; those overindulged into stupefaction roasted, but Sable and some others raced the stairs and upper floor to the balcony. Those who reached the balcony first vaulted the railing.

Sable froze and peeked below. The escapees who jumped before agonized upon the street with many broken bones or died on impact as more joined those numbers. She glanced behind. The fire she started encroached as it consumed the rest of the wood.

I may die if I do, definitely if I don't.

With a racing heart, Sable jumped onto the pile of bodies and sprained her right ankle upon Crystabella's neck before tumbling to the stones.

How am I still alive?!

Sable looked around at the horrors of war and checked her mobility. Every body part ached, worst being her ankle, as she crawled to a broken wagon and hoisted herself upon its dead horse before standing with her left leg. Sable cried. *I never thought I'd see my home like this!* After clearing her vision, Sable searched the wagon's dead coachman, found their old iron dagger in a sheath and wrapped it across herself.

"To where do I go?" Sable peered down the street toward her house where soldiers from both sides fought; then to the pitch black alleys in the direction of the Starkton Trade Company building by Titan Bay landlocked by Robert Bilteen's navy. *I need to hide.* Sable crouched into the shadows of the first alley, leaning against a stone wall with knife drawn. Creeping slow and in silence, she reached the next street undetected and peeked in the direction of commotion.

Pickpockets were stabbing and mugging a bald man with a frosted gold beard. *Mace Doran finally getting what's been coming to him!* Sable smirked. *But why is he dressed like Rhaelyn the Honeyed?* Sable staggered to the next alley and crept within the shadows, continuing her dark, painful trek until it led her to the docks of Titan Bay.

The bay was peaceful compared to the rest of the city despite being blocked by war galleys, a floating city suspended by the oil-black sea. No damage from trebuchet boulders or scorpion harpoons desecrated Titan Bay's docks, nor were any dead or dying soldiers and civilians littering the cobblestones as Robert Bilteen's buccaneers garrisoned the piers. *What an upstanding leader,* Sable realized with easing breaths. *Unless he's just keeping peace to protect his sister.* Starkton Trade Company's front porch remained lifeless excluding the faint candlelight creeping from the window near the door before it was extinguished. *Marigold has to be taking shelter in the office.*

Sable glanced to the piers and surroundings again, kept to the shadows and hid from Robert Bilteen's forces as she approached her business' front door; it smelled like smoked pork. She slid her key into the keyhole pressing one tine at a time before opening the door in silence. "Marigold?" Sable whispered to her best friend. Sable peeked around. Nothing was visible except blinding darkness while the scent of smoked pork strengthened. "It is I, Sable Wyvern, coming to hide with you."

"Thank Verítamor you're safe." Marigold tapped on the table where she sat. "I just finished reheating some hickory-smoked pork butt. Would you like some?"

"Where did you get it?" Sable asked before grabbing a chair, sitting down, and propping up her sprained ankle. "And why are you eating in the dark?"

"I've been surviving on my own this whole time, and only light fires as needed."

"Your brother's men surround us."

"He serves Alysse whereas I support Drake. I don't know whether or not he'd hold me hostage to appease her, or I'd rather remain free."

Sable's eyes adjusted. She reached before Marigold's silhouette and cut off a chunk of the meat on the plate. "Her brothel lit aflame by a fallen candle on the rushes." Sable started eating.

"You're kidding."

"It's why I'm no longer there."

"Did anyone else survive?"

"I don't know, but many within died to the flames or the streets."

"The streets?!"

Sable finished eating. "Fighting has escalated. Don't be-"

Boards on the front porch creaked. The ladies ducked below the table in silence.

"Who knows what fate is in store for us," Marigold whispered as she crawled to Sable's desk. Loud footsteps pounded the boards outside the window, followed by voices. "The trapdoor is our best bet until peace is restored."

"Agreed."

Sable joined Marigold's descent within the concealed crawlspace, moving a chair over the trapdoor to better cover their tracks. What little moonlight reflecting over the trapdoor outlined it before the ladies...

Until it reopened to light at a distant tunnel Sable traversed. The iron armor she wore was heavier than the leather vestments she wore during practice. Sable peered around the mossed stone tunnel. "Where is my horse?" questioning the light through the slits in her helmet's visor. "My ankle aches. Why must I walk without it?"

"Chance's already waiting for you." a boyish herald responded from the opening. A slender silhouette leaned beneath the arch holding a lance and shield.

"Richard, I wish you would have let me ride Chance through the tunnel." Not one hair grew upon the boy's face.

"Rules are rules, after all." He handed her the wooden lance and shield. "Remember to keep your face hidden; youth aren't allowed to compete, and mom thinks we're in the seats."

"Who cares so long as I win? I want to be the first eleven year-old girl to win Long Harvest's jousting competition. And I still can't believe we tricked her into taking us to the tournament!" She stepped onto the coliseum's spring-soaked field to a roaring mass of spectators sheltered by honeysuckled roofing and climbed upon her shire's broken-in saddle. Sable leaned against Chance's mane to his ear and whispered "may we prove those foolish girls at home wrong, my friend." *I hope Abby can see me.* Richard strode to her side as they watched a steel-armored knight hop onto a dotted thoroughbred at the other competitors' tunnel.

Their herald, a black-skinned warlock whose peregrine robe was dotted with sewn-on stars and matched the knight's gambeson, grabbed the glass pipe at his hip and roared, "All hail the Starry Knight of the Lortnok Swamp, warrior of the Perspicacious Order descended from the Patriots of Dragon Fall!"

Sable scanned the cheering crowd. Neither Winifred nor Abelot could be seen as Richard squeaked "Before you com-"

"Speak up, boy! We can't hear you!" someone yelled, followed by more of the same from other spectators. They silenced their plea as the warlock brisk-walked to Richard, knelt with the boy in prayer, and placed his hand upon Richard's shoulder once they arose.

Richard's voice magnified "Before you comes Sable Wyvern, granddaughter of Leggeron the Stern. She works when others slack, choosing success over being ordinary!" The crowd roared Sable's name, and the warlock approached her.

When he reached Sable, he whispered "Either you're brave, or foolish, girl. I know more about you than they do. Make *him* proud." before rejoining his cohort.

Doo, DOO! Doo, DOOOOO! The cornets blared with referee flags waving to begin this round. Sable's ankle ached with sharp pain as she spurred her steed to match the Starry Knight's pace and struggled to aim her lance toward his shield. Sweat and springtime humidity covered her small body beneath the cheap heavy armor and the extra leather layer clinging against her. Once the competitors met midfield, Sable ducked beneath the Starry Knight's lance and drove her lance's tip into his breastplate before almost falling off her horse from the impact when riding past.

"One, zero!" the referee exclaimed. The crowd began chanting Sable's name…

And so did Marigold Bilteen.

Sable opened her eyes to daylight flooding through the opening trapdoor and grabbed her dagger. "If today is the day I die, then I will go in self-defense!"

"I highly doubt it," called Drake Sterling as he swung the door fully open. "It wouldn't be difficult to put two prone ladies out of their misery with my sword, and I'm not here to harm you."

"You're alive!" Marigold cried with a smile as she reached to Drake's hand.

Drake pulled her out of the crawlspace and responded, "Yes, ladies" while helping Marigold to her feet.

He then reached to Sable who leaned against her desk away from her sprained ankle, leaning with her away from his bandaged knee. Pink sunlight from the window and open door stung her eyes focused on the Grey Foxes guarding the porch. "Is it over?" she asked him.

"Almost. Come with me." The ladies followed him outside to the crowd of survivors and Robert Bilteen's unarmed soldiers huddling before the piers garrisoned by Drake's Grey Foxes. A husky, bald-headed man with a thick, greying gold beard knelt on the pier where *Silver Hare* was docked. Drake walked onto the pier, but as Sable and Marigold attempted to follow, the soldiers barred their path and commanded them to join the others. Drake Sterling stood beside the man. The crowd silenced.

"When the plague struck us, my father, your king, was amongst those who succumbed to it. My mother, your queen, sought to disrespect his legacy and my traditional claim to the throne by buying the loyalty of turncoats and entertaining the sins of this wicked world as we good people of Starkton battled pestilence and war. My silent benefactors noticed peculiarities. To those amongst us who visited her brothel, did you notice how not one of her whores contracted the illness despite fornicating with who knows how many degenerates? To those amongst us who cheered as she financed you without labor, do you know where the money originated? My counsellors and I suspect witchcraft took place behind closed doors as you were distracted." Tears built within Drake's lacrimal glands and watered his eyes. With a cracked voice, he continued, "But now I believe my mother faced a witch's fate when her fort was razed last night. She and High King Lesirion Strigil's forces retaliated after the brothel started burning, but the opportunity ended in our favor when my father's allies turned the tide of battle and I slew the High King and cleansed Starkton's streets. Because of their end, I am now both your King and Lantheon's High King." He turned his gaze to the man beside him. "However, Mace Doran's body was discovered amongst the dead, and Rickard Bilteen was slain alongside the High King, thus leaving Randall's final son Robert being the last known surviving rebel leader." The new high king drew his sword. "What say you his fate?"

"Behead the traitor!" the majority roared.

Marigold and Sable shook with fear. "He does not deserve this!" Sable exclaimed to Marigold. "Help your brother!"

"YOUR GRACE!" Marigold called. "YOUR GRACE!" She stepped to the pier and was blocked by Grey Foxes. "Step aside!" she commanded.

"We don't take orders from you." one sneered.

Drake saw the exchange, commanding "Let her through" unto the soldiers. They stepped aside in reluctance, and Marigold waved to Sable, following without further incident.

Sable stared into the purple, hardened eyes of the gruff captain whose life she now held in her hands. *He looks like a heavyset version of Randall.* The crowd silenced again. "Robert, when I slipped into the harbor undetected last night, this region of the city was in tranquility. How did you preserve such order amongst chaos?"

"I do my best to do unto others as I want in return, and no one dared attack my fleet or soldiers." Robert's eyes turned to the king. "Everyone here is my neighbor just as yours."

"During this civil war, were you involved with any battles whatsoever?"

"None, my lady. I simply held Titan Bay as commanded by Queen Alysse."

"So you are well-acquainted with loyalty?" *Just like your father?*

"Yes."

"So, if our new king was to command perpetual fealty, with your sons to serve as his stewards and cupbearers until they come of age to knighthood, you would not dispute this alternative?"

Robert's eye lit with hope. "Correct, my lady."

High King Drake sheathed his sword. "The matter is settled without bloodshed. Arise, my new Naval Master, as I command unto thee those atonements as stated by our famed musician, Sable Wyvern, before the people of Starkton." The cheers of those who supported Drake's decision overwhelmed the disdain from those steadfast for further violence as Robert rose to his feet and bowed unto the crowd. Robert walked to Sable, hugged and thanked her for saving his life before reuniting with his sister.

David S. Longworth

The sunlight rippled upon Titan Bay as High King Drake Sterling announced, "Good people of Starkton, this matter was one of the final loose ends for us to tie besides locating our beloved hero, Sir Abelot Wyvern the Golden Dragon, who disappeared after the Latran Wolves turned the tide of last night's battle in our favor; but rest assured, I am confident he will turn up stronger than ever. In the meantime, let's rebuild Starkton as a better city than my parents left it." The crowd's roaring cheers echoed throughout Starkton.

ALEIKUM ES SELAMU

Golden rays illuminated High King Drake Sterling's bedchamber and reflected off the treasures his parents left behind and a silver harp sitting upon a table, awakening the sleeping king. As he began to stretch, his crippled leg throbbed with knives piercing his knee and its surrounding tendons and muscles. "Five years of dealing with this pain for the greater good," the king grumbled whilst shaking his auburn bedhead and extending his knee in repetition until it popped. "The Second Hop of the Rabbits, they call it…" He looked to the cane beside his folded clothes on the nightstand. "…And I can't even hop anymore."

"…h-Huh?" Sable Wyvern rustled from beneath the covers.

More rustling ensued from Drake's other side. "You grouching about your leg again, Honey?" inquired High Queen

Marigold Bilteen-Sterling. "I wish it would heal like Sable's ankle did. Don't forget to eat your medicinal cake sent from the monk in Dragon Fall."

Sable gave a brief lick to her lips. "We need more cakes. They help my creativity and make sex better too." She patted Drake's manhood. Her eyes sparkled. "Say, I could go for another round."

A mischievous smile crept beneath Drake's beard. "Me too. What about y-"

The bedchamber's door swung open without a knock.

Are you kidding me?! Drake cursed in silence and scowled. A young girl and boy wearing nightgowns stormed into the room, their bare feet patting across the floor before they jumped onto the bed and wrapped their arms around Sable while she and Marigold kept the majority of their bodies covered; the girl hugged tighter than the boy.

"Auntie, Auntie," they screeched from their innocent smiles. The boy's purple eyes and girl's sapphire eyes shined as Drake controlled his breathing and mussed their brown hair.

Sable made eye contact with the younglings and started brushing her fingers through the girl's hair. "Ash and Phoenikas, what are you two doing running around the castle wearing your nightclothes? Is this how good children behave at home?"

"We he' voices in the 'cheh woom,'" Ash informed them.

"It's called the throne room, not 'chair room,'" Sable scolded just as an irritated mother would. "Say 'throne room' and correct your pronunciation."

"I'm sowwy. Thwone woom," Ash whispered in embarrassment.

"That was better, but still not perfect; work on your pronunciation." Sable looked at Phoenikas again. "Now it's your turn."

"Thwone woom."

"Ugh!" Sable bowed her head in frustration for a couple seconds before meeting eyes with Phoenikas again. "Same task for you. Now younglings, return to your guestroom and get dressed. And I mean it."

The children responded in unison "yes Auntie" before they left the room.

High Queen Marigold uncovered herself, closed and locked the door, and dressed herself in silence as did Sable. *Why did we forget to do that last night?* High King Drake made the bed, creasing each corner of the bedding to perfect square angles while his wife watched in frustration and handed him his cane. *If only we were not interrupted.* "I hate people."

"No, you don't," the queen exclaimed. "If you did, then you would not have slept with us last night nor become King of Starkton and High King of the Lantheon Realm. You need your morning coffee."

"Good idea." Drake snapped his fingers and clapped his hands for a few seconds to an unnamed tune the jesters of his boyhood jingled from the bells ornamenting their costume. "Sable, get us all some coffee once you tend to your niece and nephew."

Sable's confusion caused by Drake's behavior broke. "Yes, Your Grace," she responded with a nod.

"I want mine…"

"Pardon me, Your Grace." Sable walked to the table where a feather leaning in an inkwell laid next to stacked paper sheets and pulled one off the stack. She then wiped the excess ink off the sides of the feather's sharpened tip before bringing it to the paper. "I'm ready now."

"I want mine plain, dark, and strong enough to keep me alert all day," Drake ordered. His stomach grumbled to the delicate scratching of the ink feather. "And two bacon-egg-and-cheese biscuits to accompany it."

High Queen Marigold squint her eyes to the king. "I want hot spiced cider, and the same type of biscuits.

Drake commented "Don't forget to get yourself and the children something too."

"Thank you, Your Grace." Sable wrote her silent wishes, dried the ink with her breath, and left the room with royal orders in hand.

Marigold gave a tender grasp to Drake's thick arm after they stepped into the hallway and locked the bedchamber's door. "You're awfully tender with Abelot and Samantha's children; they are not our own. Why is this?" Drake freed his arm and hobbled for the throne room. "Your Grace, please do not deny me truth."

Drake's eyes never met his wife's as they continued their diligent trek. He winced with each agonizing step of his crippled leg.

"Is this how a woman speaks of children not from her own womb, your best friend's niece and nephew nonetheless?" *I owe protection and provision to the children and sister of the hero who saved my kingdom. I would adopt them if either Lady Starlight or Sable asked of me and leave them in my will just as I would our would-be brood.* "And you ask me this after I offered them food?"

"You're right. I should not have done that."

Snobbish voices echoed throughout the throne room and down the halls. *Maybe they didn't hear any part of our discussion; the last thing I need is someone trying to start another feud for me to deal with.* Those voices succumbed unto obedient silence as the pompous aristocrats eyed Starkton's monarchs. *Spoiled, self-righteous good-for-nothings surround me.* Drake's nose curled. *How many of them bathed in perfume at this hour?* "Good morning." His gaze met several faces. "I pray at least one of you has come to bring good news this morning; I need something worthwhile to compliment my impending coffee."

A feminine man, dressed in a bright raspberry silk robe and women's house slippers, slithered from the edge of the crowd before the throne, citrus and honeysuckle perfume preceding him. "Your Grace, first and foremost may your morning shine like sunshine on the sea," he purred whilst patting and combing out with gentle fingers tangles in his wavy sun-dyed locks. "And, thank you for this new position as 'Keeper of Whispers,' though 'Queen of Whispers' sounds better." His doe eyes sparkled like stars.

The high king's nose further curled as this licentious man paused to break eye contact and rubbed his hands with powder out of the woman's satchel he wore. "Jasmine…," Drake coughed, "…state your business."

"I heard from the other working ladies there have been no whispers of treachery in the streets of Starkton."

Sable entered the throne room carrying a silver platter bearing the king and queen's breakfast.

"Where's yours?" the king asked.

"I ate mine fast enough for your meal to arrive still warm, Your Grace. I asked the cooks and servants to keep the children in order while they still eat, if you don't mind."

"Well done, and that is fine with me." Drake sat the plate on his lap and sipped his coffee as High Queen Marigold grabbed her biscuits and cider before she left. He then turned back to the tranny. "Have you anything regarding Mace Doran's conniving mother?" He started eating the biscuits.

"During the King's Plague pandemic, an elderly woman matching her description was recorded in the chapel's necrology manifesto; however, neither the gemstone bow nor dagger resurfaced since those weapons vanished during your battle against your mother and the last High King."

The king took a strong sip of his coffee, embracing the vitality it granted. "Speaking of alliances, have you any news from across the sea?" Drake finished eating his last biscuit and turned to Sable Wyvern. "Or even of the Golden Dragon?"

Jasmine misted powder before him with a clap. "Ever since Emperor Septimius' assassin eliminated Davirius and your uncle cleansed the sea of that water moccasin Nolryk, no one has dared to challenge Marilyn Yor's sovereignty over Pylon, and House Doran seems to be no more unless any of them somehow cheated death." Jasmine turned to Sable. "Unfortunately, no one has seen Abelot-"

Sable stormed out the throne room, shaking her head and sobbing as tears filled her eyes.

"Poor lady, I can only imagine the pain of losing one brother and the other going missing. As I was saying, no one has seen Abelot or his Morning Glory since the great battle; however, a survivor of the battle claimed they saw his bastard blade transform into a golden great sword, matching his signature armor, when Abelot laid his unicorn to rest. The same claimant thought they heard him dub this new version of Morning Glory as 'Dragon Fire.'"

"Gold like his armor, you say? We'll have to test this claim when Starkton's Golden Dragon makes himself known again." High King Drake finished drinking his coffee. "I cannot think of any other topics of interest. Have you no further information needing to be brought to my attention?"

"Not at the moment, Your Grace."

Good, you gossiping wretch. "You're excused to engage your other business."

Jasmine bowed. "Thank you for today's opportunity, Your Grace," Jasmine purred before he departed the throne room.

"Does anyone else have anything requiring my immediate attention?"

All at once, the remaining aristocrats flooded the atmosphere with industrial news, pleas for amendments, and trial announcements, so High King Drake Sterling directed nearby servants to endure their babbling after he left the room. Quietness within the hall leading to his bedchamber returned tranquility to his mind and soul when it drowned the chaos left behind.

Drake unlocked the door and looked at the table. "She's gone back to town," he murmured to the spot on the table where Sable's silver harp laid earlier. *Starkton Trade Company, for her duties there?* "As I lead, so I follow." Drake exited the bedchamber, relocked its door, and headed to the courtyard where his late father's carriage idled horseless until he commanded the White and Grey Keep's stable master to horse it before climbing into the cabin.

CHUN! Clip. Clap. Clop. Clup. Clip. Clap. Clop. Clup. The carriage began its journey from the White and Grey Keep to the city of Starkton. No one sat in the carriage's cabin with High King Drake, so all he could do was embrace the serenity of Starkton's countryside and venture within the labyrinth of his mind.

Drake closed his eyes and retreated within.

His carriage disappeared as he was left in solitude to stroll through a wheat field some of the local farmers maintained for market. Drake's stroll brought him to a tree where he broke off a branch, pulled a long string from one of his pockets, and dug with a rock for night crawlers to tie to one end of the string and the branch on the other. Once he assembled his fishing rod, Drake started fishing the still part of the castle's moat.

CHUN! The carriage stopped.

The high king opened his eyes. He was outside the open stone archway gapping the stone walls of Wyvern's Courtyard, the former location of Alysse's Brothel, being greeted by the salvaged dragon statue and vegetation. Drake Sterling exited the carriage and limped through the stone archway replacing the Lilan-themed door that stood there years ago.

Not one leaf protruded past the stone walls from apple and peach trees planted where dens of impiety once edified within the walls, for limbs growing against those walls were trimmed to perfection by Starkton's most disciplined gardeners. Shaded by the fruit trees were stone benches and tall fescue grass growing around and between stone trails pathed from the remnants of stones once walked by heathens. Surrounded by children and dogs playing as their parents watched from the benches, Drake approached the unshaded dragon statue. His peripherals stung when he got closer to a shining object at the dragon's feet.

The king covered his stinging peripherals to discover a sword sheathed within a gilt scabbard infused with orange swirls. "Is this what I think this is?!" King Drake exclaimed as he grabbed its hilt and unsheathed the great sword. Squinting, he covered part of the fuller with his hands to block the excess sunlight. "This blade matches Jasmine's description of Dragon Fire." *Who put Dragon Fire where someone could find it after all these years?* Drake sheathed the sword, wrapped the scabbard with his removed shirt, and embraced the summer warmth upon his bare torso. "Today feels like a good day to v-"

CR-R-RUNCH!!!

Drake jumped up and turned to a V-shaped tree surrounded by boys. He grabbed the sword and limped with it to the tree. "What have you miscreants done?" King Drake called out.

"We told you girls can't do boy things," a boy who didn't turn to the king teased.

Another one noticed King Drake and yelled. "Let's get outta here!" The boys then took off and left behind a young girl sitting in a dirt pile holding a thin branch long enough to substitute for a child's wooden sword.

"Sweet little Phoenikas, what are you doing breaking branches off trees and dirtying your pretty dress?" *This branch didn't fall far from Abelot Wyvern's family tree.*

"I wanted to pway with them 'cause Ash won't pway with me."

Drake scanned the courtyard for Ash Wyvern. "Where is he?"

Phoenikas pointed to a lone tree. "He was wast sitting with his eyes closed."

Ash doesn't need to be wasting his youth. "Why?"

"Thinking and wouldn't say."

Ash could go places if he gets his mind right when he comes of age. "Where is he now?"

"He wanted to go back to Auntie before sitting under the tree."

"Is an adult here to take care of you?"

"We snuck out."

"I see." *I may need to get the city guards to keep him safe.* "You can get in a lot of trouble if you're not careful." Drake winced at his throbbing leg. "Come with me." They went to where Drake found Dragon Fire. He sat where the sword was and placed it on his lap. "This sword can hurt someone. Did you see who left this sword here?"

Phoenikas shook her head.

"Thank you." Drake grabbed the hilt of his cane and pointed its tip to the girl. "I promise to watch over you and take you home when you're ready to go." He extended to Phoenikas. "En garde!"

Phoenikas held the branch with both hands, pointed its tip to the king and gave an innocent smile. "Thank you, Uncle King!"

King Drake smiled in return. "You're welcome."

They played sword fighting with their wooden "weapons." Phoenikas kept eyeing the sword as she was smacking Drake's cane with her branch and scoring periodic hits. "I heard my daddy was a knight with a sword. Is that one mine?"

High King Drake Sterling smiled ear to ear and chimed "Not yet, Little Dragon."

AFTERWORD

Thank you for spending your time, the most valuable currency anyone can offer to another in mortal life, to read *A King's Wisdom*; every aspect of this book has been similar to wrangling a ferocious beast barehanded and unarmored. And I give unending thanks to my fans waiting since *A Lord's Treasure* was published in January 2018!

Starting with combining two different book ideas into one with direction, *A King's Wisdom* was originally intended to be an educational Dark Medieval Fantasy series, with its first volume *A Lord's Treasure* focusing on personal finance, second volume focusing on philosophy with possible title *A Knight's Philosophy*, and so on until everything wrapped up. However, I wasn't satisfied with *A Lord's Treasure* and the limiting direction of the original idea, so I reworked the series by combining the reworked *A Lord's Treasure* story with the newer chapters until I created a book I could consider my "magnum opus" unless another claims that honor.

Speaking of honors…

Foremost, I wish to thank the Supreme Architect of the Universe for the countless blessings, protection, guidance, and forgiveness He's granted and has in store for me.

Second, I wish to thank my Brethren and guys at the gym who kept me pursuing my highest potential in life instead of succumbing to mediocrity and complacency.

Third, I wish to thank everyone who has taken the initiative to be a blessing and supportive to me instead of a curse.

Finally, I wish to thank everyone who has been involved directly and indirectly with getting this book on shelves. Without your input, this book would not reach those who are supposed to read it.

- David Longworth
   April 14, 2024

David S. Longworth is a freelance writer, entrepreneur, and philanthropist living in the Winston-Salem region of North Carolina. After earning his Bachelor's in Business Administration double-majored in Management and Marketing and minored in Supply Chain Management from Appalachian State University in 2015, he has dedicated his life to continual self-improvement and being an influential role model for people on the Autism Spectrum. Longworth has written articles for Appalachian State University's *Club Sports Illustrated* publication, created advertisements which have appeared in *The Elkin Tribune*, and is an avid reader and athlete.

www.linkedin.com/in/davidlongworth1
www.author-davidlongworth.com

www.ingramcontent.com/pod-product-compliance
Lightning Source LLC
Chambersburg PA
CBHW031102020726
47495CB00007B/1999